For Carle

I hope

these school stories. Enjoy!

Kay S. Heath

Ida Claire,
That's Funny!

Seventh Printing

Written by:
Kay Strickland Heath

Illustrated by:
Jan Alston

Ida Claire, That's Funny!

Written by:
Kay Strickland Heath

Illustrated by:
Jan Alston

To order additional copies of her books, or to discuss
speaking engagements, please contact the author directly:
Kay S. Heath
906 Pine Avenue
Dawson, GA 39842
Email:kayheath@mchsi.com

PUBLISHED BY:
BRENTWOOD ACADEMIC PRESS
4000 BEALLWOOD AVENUE
COLUMBUS, GEORGIA 31904

Dedication

I dedicate this book to my Mama, Gertrude Strickland. She has always been my encourager. By her words and through her actions, she has taught me the importance of laughing, of listening, and of loving. I am very fortunate to be her daughter!

First book by author: *Ida Claire, It's Summertime!*

Acknowledgements

I appreciate the many readers of *Ida Claire, It's Summertime!* who expressed to me that I needed to write a sequel.

I owe a debt of gratitude to Martha Spurlock. She is my mentor, my friend, and a former teacher. Her suggestions and corrections of this manuscript have been valuable.

Thank you to my talented friend, Jan Alston. She gives this book extra life through her wonderful pictures.

I offer a huge "thank you" to my family and friends who were willing to share a memory, an idea, or a story that contributed to this book. These include Jaimie Murdock, Rhonda Brown, Betty Heath, Johnny Heath, Mike Adams, Clay Miller, Diane Strickland, Ann Chambless, Leon Strickland, Gertrude Strickland, Leann H. Miller, Sandee Ortega, Tyler Dorminey, and Sally Loska.

After teaching primary grades for thirty years, I have memories of students that leave an impression. Most of my students were wonderful kids. A few were unique and challenging. Some of the characters in this book have been created from observations of former students. Of course, names have been changed to protect the innocent (and the guilty). A heartfelt "thank you" goes to each student I taught, especially to the ones that kept things interesting!

Introduction

It is time for Will to go to school for the first time. He enjoys learning about letters and numbers. But, he really likes finding out about the other kids in his class. Ida Claire has already told him about different ones that he might meet. She says that every class has a bully, a sissy, a crybaby, and a tattletale. Will discovers each one of these types and more! He also meets some really funny boys! Each day brings a new and fun experience that he shares with Ida Claire after school.

Table of Contents

Chapter 1

First Things First

That first day of school was just as scary as I thought it would be. I'm not talking about the kind of scary like somebody jumping out from behind a door and saying "Boo!" I mean the kind of scary that feels like frogs jumping trying to catch the butterflies flying around in your stomach. I told Ida Claire how I felt and she said that I was just a little nervous. But, shoot, I was more than nervous. I was scared to death!

Ida Claire was my cousin. We were lucky. We lived next door to each other and we were best friends. Our Mamas were sisters. Mama, Aunt Ima, Ida Claire, and I all went to my class first. I already knew that Mrs. Dunn was my teacher because Ida Claire showed me my name listed in Mrs. Dunn's class when it was in the newspaper.

The first thing I saw on the door was a picture of a red school house and some letters that said W-E-L-C-O-M-E! I could read some words, but not that one. We stepped through the doorway and a lady bent over me and smiled. She said, "You must be Will Lee. Welcome to first grade. My name is Mrs. Dunn. See if you can find your desk. It will have your name on it."

I said, "Yes, Ma'am." Then I turned around to look at Ida Claire. I knew she would help me find my desk. Mrs.

Dunn asked Ida Claire if she had a nice summer. Ida Claire said, "Yes, Ma'am, Will and I had some great adventures."

Mrs. Dunn said, "I'm sure you did!" I didn't know how she knew about our summer. Then she said, "Maybe Will can tell us about some of the fun things you did during the summer when we have share time later." I decided right then that I liked Mrs. Dunn!

Ida Claire and I walked around the room looking at all the name tags on the desks. She pointed to one and I said, "Yep, that's mine." Then I sat down. Mama came over to see where I was sitting. She said, "We'll go take Ida Claire to her third grade classroom. I know you'll have a great day! I'll see you this afternoon." I looked up at her and thought about that earlier that morning I meant to tell her not to kiss me good-bye. Mama's eyes looked kind of watery but she didn't bend down to kiss me. Thank goodness! She just waved and smiled. Whew! After all, I was in first grade now and I didn't want any of the boys in my class to think I was a sissy.

When Ida Claire got to the door, she yelled back to me, "Maybe I'll see you on the playground at recess or in the cafeteria at lunch, Will."

Now some other boys and girls and their Mamas were coming in to the room. I got up out of my desk and walked to a table that had books spread out on top. I heard Mrs. Dunn say that we could look at the books while we waited for everybody to get to school. I picked out a book about trains. Since my Daddy worked for the railroad, I always wanted to look at pictures of trains. When I got back to my desk, I heard somebody crying at the door. I looked and saw a little girl with her head buried in her Mama's dress. She was sniffling and wiping her eyes and her runny nose. I reckon she was really scared or either she had gotten her finger mashed in the car door or something.

Mrs. Dunn kneeled down to her and asked, "What is your name?" The little girl just buried her head in her Mama's dress again. The lady told her that the little girl was named Ethel Lewis. Mrs. Dunn put her hand on Ethel's shoulder and said, "Let's find your desk, okay?"

The desks were set up two in a row and they were almost in a circle. Really they were in the shape of a horseshoe with the open end facing the blackboard. I knew a horseshoe was supposed to mean Good Luck. But, it turns out it wasn't very lucky for me because Ethel Lewis's name was on the desk right behind mine. She sat down in her desk and Mrs. Dunn got a chair for Ethel's Mama to sit beside her. I didn't know how long Ethel's Mama would stay there. I reckon Ethel didn't care if anybody thought she was a sissy or a crybaby. But after they sat down, at least she got quiet.

All the boys and girls that were in our class so far were staring at Ethel. That meant they were looking toward me too! It was sort of quiet. Then, all of a sudden I heard a noise at the door of our room. I looked up and saw a boy that had dirt smeared on his face. He must not have had a comb. And I know he hadn't been to the barbershop for a haircut all summer. His shirttail was half way hanging out. The cuff of one blue jean leg was rolled up half way and the other one was touching the ground. He was barefooted and grinning. Mrs. Dunn asked him his name. He took two steps into the room and in a loud voice he said, "My name is Levi Mullins. I'm here at school so I can learn how to read today!" He held up his hand. He was clutching a big bullfrog and then he said, "I caught this bullfrog this morning while I was waiting on the school bus! I thought maybe I could play with it here at school. He's going to be my new pet!"

That started Ethel to crying again. Her Mama was patting her and telling her, "Sh-sh-sh." Two girls ran to the windows to get away from the frog or from Levi or from both. Mrs. Dunn raised her hands up in the air. And I sort of grinned. It looked to me like this first day of school might not be too scary after all. I thought maybe it would be fun for sure!

Chapter 2

One Thing after Another

That bullfrog sure did cause a commotion in the room. But, Mrs. Dunn seemed to know what to do to get things back under control. She walked to Levi and put both of her hands on his shoulders. She guided him over to the cabinet and opened the door. She said, "Levi, I'm going to let you put your new little pet in this empty shoebox. At recess you can get him a rock and some grass to go in his house. We'll put a saucer of water in there for him, too. But the way he hops, he might turn that saucer over." Then Mrs. Dunn took a pair of scissors and jabbed some holes in the lid of the shoebox. She pulled out a big rubber band. She told Levi, "If you want to, you can put your frog in the little stream that runs at the back of the playground when we go outside for recess."

Levi said, "I don't think I can do that Teacher because he'll be homesick for the creek close to where I found him." Levi put the frog in the box and Mrs. Dunn put the lid and the rubber band on the box. She took the box and put it on the shelf that was above some hooks on the wall. Mrs. Dunn told Levi that she would help him to find his desk.

Levi's desk was to the side of mine. He sorta stepped into the seat of his desk. Both feet were in his desk where his bottom was supposed to be. He looked over at me and said, "I'm gonna name that bullfrog Hoppy! Don't you think that will be a good name for him? What's your name?"

I told him, "My name is Will Lee. I reckon Hoppy will be a good name!"

About that time we heard a deep voice coming from a tall, skinny man standing at the door. He put out his hand to shake hands with Mrs. Dunn. Then he said, "My name is Bob Seay. That's spelled S-e-a-y, but it's pronounced like the letter "C". And this is my son, A.B." Mr. Seay's voice was so deep it almost sounded like thunder rolling. Mr. Seay said, "Tell Mrs. Dunn 'Good morning', A.B."

A.B. looked around the class and then he looked up at Mrs. Dunn. He said, "Good morning, Mrs. Dunn." I noticed right off that his voice had a whine in it. He talked real slow and he sounded like his nose was stopped up real bad. If Mama or Aunt Ima had heard him talking, they would have told him to go blow his nose. Every now and then he sniffed. But no matter how much he sniffed, he still sounded clogged up to me.

Behind me I heard Ethel say to her Mama, "He needs to use a handkerchief to blow his nose." By that time she was coloring a page that Mrs. Dunn had torn out of a coloring book. Mrs. Dunn told us that a little box of Crayola crayons was in everybody's desk and she put a page from the coloring book on each desk.

I looked at Levi and he was still squatting on his feet in his desk. I don't think he knew about trying to stay inside the lines while he was coloring. But he knew about speed. His paper had one color on it. Brown scribbled lines covered the whole page. He hollered, "Teacher, I'm finished with this one. Can I have another picture to color pretty?"

Mrs. Dunn said, "Yes, of course, but you need to take your time, Levi!" Then, she smiled at Ethel's mama and A.B.'s daddy. A.B.'s daddy said that he needed to leave to get to work but he wanted to know how much lunch money he needed to pay. Mrs. Dunn said, "It's twenty cents a day, so you can pay a dollar for the week." Mr. Seay gave Mrs. Dunn the money, waved good-by to A.B. and left.

I forgot all about lunch until they mentioned the money. I was glad Mama made me eat a good breakfast because all the boys and girls hadn't gotten there yet. I figured we couldn't eat lunch until they all came to school.

A boy named Gillie Dunbar and his mama came through the door of our school room next. Gillie wore glasses and was real skinny. He sorta stayed real close to his mama. Mrs. Dunn showed him his desk. His mama walked over to his desk and told him, "Gillie, sit down and be my good little boy all day today. Don't get your new school clothes dirty, and be sure to eat everything on your plate at lunch. I'll come back to pick you up this afternoon." Gillie sniffed and wiped under his nose with the back of his hand. Then he put his head on his folded arms on top of his desk. His mama unsnapped her pocketbook, took out a Kleenex, held the tissue under Gillie's nose, and said, "Blow hard!" Then she kissed the top of his head and patted it.

Whew! I sure was glad that Gillie's mama wasn't my mama. I was pretty sure that Gillie was gonna be the sissy in our class. Last week when Ida Claire was talking about school to me, she said that every class always has a boy that is a sissy. She said, "He's the one that won't get his hands dirty because he doesn't know how to play and have fun at recess. He's also the one that will be chicken to do stuff." I reckon Ida Claire was pretty smart because she was already in third grade. I knew this afternoon I'd be able to tell her about the boys and girls in my class. I was pretty sure that she would agree with me that Gillie Dunbar was our sissy.

I didn't hear all the boys' and girls' names in our room, but I heard Mrs. Dunn say, "We have twenty of our students here now. In just a few more minutes we'll start our regular day. Look at the clock. The time is nine o'clock. Tomorrow we'll be busy working at this time." I looked at the clock. But I couldn't tell time so it's a good thing she told me it was nine o'clock. I thought about when I used to be at home at this time every morning. When the clock looked the way it does now, it was time for Captain Kangaroo. I loved to watch the Captain and all his friends. I liked Mr. Green Jeans, Mr. Moose, and Bunny Rabbit. Then I thought to myself: I reckon I'll find out tomorrow what will be taking the place of Captain Kangaroo every day!

Chapter 3

It Takes All Kinds

Before Mrs. Dunn could start the almost regular day, two more students came to the door. I remembered seeing both of them for the first time but not for the same reasons. The first one was a girl. She came skipping into the room. She had on a green dress and Mary Jane shoes. She said, "My name is Maggie Mae Warren." She looked up at Mrs. Dunn and smiled. She had hair that hung down in little curls on her shoulders and pretty green eyes. She even had freckles on her nose. She was prettier than any puppy I'd ever seen. I thought about that I'd have to be sure to tell Ida Claire about her. But I couldn't tell anybody else because they wouldn't understand. Maggie Mae must have already known Ethel. She raised her shoulders, waved a little wave at her and said, " Hey." Now I was glad that Ethel was behind me because I got to look straight at Maggie Mae.

Ethel's mama must have thought it was a good time to leave. She told Ethel, "Look, there's your friend Maggie Mae. You can show her the pretty picture you colored." Then she went out the door.

Virgil Acworth was the other boy that came through the door. He was taller than any of the rest of us. He glanced around the room and scuffed across the floor to one of the first desks. He sat down and then slumped down in his desk. He acted like he had been in this room before that morning. He had squinty-looking eyes that were dark. He looked sorta sneaky to me. As a matter of fact, he reminded me of Dewey. Dewey was our back door neighbor that always cheated at marbles. Dewey also said bad words sometimes. I wondered if this boy was hard-to-learn and had to stay back in first grade like Dewey did.

I'd have to find out about that later because right then Mrs. Dunn said, "Boys and girls, all of our students are here now and we will walk in line to go in the hall to the restroom. When you walk in line, you do not touch the wall, and you stay right behind the person in front of you." Then she told us to go to the door. Well, we did! We sorta all bunched together at the door. Mrs. Dunn said, "No, you need to get in the line the way your desks are in line—alphabetically." I didn't know what she meant, but I figured I would learn about that big word later. She started calling names to get us to line up right.

We walked down the hall and around the corner. Mrs. Dunn said, "This is the girls' restroom first," and she pointed to the sign. Then she pointed to the sign that had B-O-Y-S and said, "Boys, this is your rest-room." She said that three at a time could go in. Oh! When I went in, I found out that a restroom was the same as a bathroom. But, I never had seen such short little commodes. Plus, there were two funny-looking commodes hanging on the wall.

I was in there with Levi and Gillie. Levi said, "I'm gonna have a hard time squatting in that one that is hanging on the wall." I told him that he wasn't supposed to use it that way. I could tell right off that Levi had a lot more to learn about school than I did. Virgil busted into the door. Uh,oh! We were supposed to have only three. I went to the little glass bowl with pink stuff in it that was hanging on the wall between the sinks. Virgil saw me looking at it. He said, "That's soap, Dummy. If you push this silver thing up, the soap will come out in your hand. And if you want to make Mrs. Dunn mad, all you have to do is stuff those brown paper towels down into the sink drain." Then he looked at Gillie and said, "What are looking at, Four Eyes?"

Shoot, I sure didn't want to make Mrs. Dunn mad so I motioned for Levi and Gillie to come on and we went back into the hall. Everybody finished using the restrooms and Mrs. Dunn got us lined back up in the hall. I saw another class coming. I looked to see if it was Ida Claire's class. But they were all about my size. So I knew they were too little to be third graders. I saw somebody waving and saw it was Jimmy. He was my cousin. His daddy, my Uncle Jim, was my Mama's brother. Jimmy was in the other first grade room. I waved back to him. We each walked on in our line.

When we got back to the room, Mrs. Dunn said that we would find out about other parts of the school later. Then she said, "But right now I want to talk about our classroom. Let's look around the room and talk about what's on the walls." She pointed to a spot right beside the door. She said, "This is our bulletin board. Right now it has pictures of different animals with words beside each. I want you to take turns naming an animal you see and I'll tell you what we connect with that animal. Raise your hand if you want a turn."

Maggie Mae raised her hand first. When Mrs. Dunn called her name, she said, "I see a bee."

Mrs. Dunn said, "That's right, we should be *busy* as a bee in first grade!"

Another little girl named Jeannette raised her hand. She said, "I see an owl."

Mrs. Dunn said, "Good, that's right. We want to be *wise* as an owl."

Then Levi said, "Teacher, Teacher, I see a horse!"

Mrs. Dunn said, "That's right, Levi, but you need to raise your hand and you also need to get your feet out of your desk. When we see the horse, we need to remember to *work* like a horse."

A girl raised her hand. Mrs. Dunn said, "Yes, Marylou, which animal do you see?"

Marylou said, "I see a lamb."

"Yes, we should be *gentle* as a lamb," Mrs. Dunn said.

I raised my hand next. When Mrs. Dunn called on me, I said, "I see a mouse."

She said, "That's right, Will, we need to be *quiet* as a mouse sometimes." I felt good inside and I smiled. Then I happened to glance at Virgil. He had a hateful look on his face. He made sure that Mrs. Dunn wasn't looking his way. Then he balled up his hand into a fist and shook it at me. I quit looking his way and I quit smiling, too. I remembered Ida Claire telling me that a class will usually have a bully. She said that a bully always tries to boss everybody and tries to start fights. She said that he also picks on other kids. I was pretty sure that I knew who the bully was in our room—Virgil Acworth!

Chapter 4

A Different Train

The next part of the room that Mrs. Dunn wanted us to look at was a train on top of the blackboard. I saw it had words written on each train car. I knew about the engine, caboose, and box cars. But I didn't know the words written on them. Mrs. Dunn said, "These are the months of the year. I have little cards with your names on them and I will stick your name on the month you have a birthday. Let's see who knows their birthday."

She started calling each boy and girl. She said that she would call them alphabetically. So she called the first person that was at the bottom of our horseshoe-shaped desks. Most kids knew when their birthday was. Mrs. Dunn taped each card sticking out of the right train car. When she asked if I knew my birthday, I said, "Yes, Ma'am, my birthday is February 14th."

Mrs. Dunn said, "How nice! Your birthday is Valentine's Day." I kinda grinned. Ethel knew her birthday, too.

Then it was Levi's turn. She asked him if he knew his birthday. Levi said, "Well, I don't know nothing about them words on that nice train you got up there, but I know my birthday is in five more sleeps. My mama told me that this morning. Yep, she said that in five more sleeps, when I wake up that next morning, it will be my birthday!"

Mrs. Dunn smiled. Then she looked in a book she called her register and said, "That's right, Levi. Your birthday is September 9th". Then she put Levi's name card on the birthday train.

When she called A.B.'s name, he slowly turned his head and blinked. In his slow, stopped-up-nose whine sound he said, "My birthday was supposed to be last Sunday, but my mama said we couldn't have my party until next Saturday. So at my birthday party I'll turn six years old."

Mrs. Dunn cleared her throat, "A.B., your birthday was Sunday and that was September 2nd." A.B. just shrugged his shoulders and sniffed.

After Mrs. Dunn called the names of a few more boys and girls, she called Maggie Mae. I had been watching carefully to find out when her birthday was. Maggie Mae said, "My birthday is February 15th. My birthday is right after Will's." Then she pointed at me and smiled. My insides felt warm and I think my face turned red.

Mrs. Dunn checked back in that register book and looked back at the birthday train. She said, "That completes our train. Let's count how many names we have. I heard Mrs. Dunn and a few others saying the numbers. I counted every one. I sure was glad that Ida Claire had practiced counting with me yesterday.

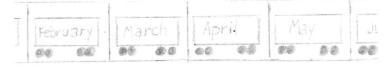

Mrs. Dunn said, "Anytime we have a birthday boy or girl, we will sing 'Happy Birthday' to them. That student will get to wear the class birthday hat." Then she said, "And they will get a birthday spanking!" She said, "A.B., you're our first birthday for September. I know today is not your birthday, but we were not in school on your exact birthday. So you need to come toward the chalkboard and stand in front of me." Slowly A.B. walked to where Mrs. Dunn was standing. He walked like he was going to a hanging in the TV western shows. He must have been thinking that he was the one going to be hanged. Mrs. Dunn put on the birthday hat and we sang "Happy Birthday" to A.B. Then she jerked her hand way back and acted like she was going to spank him hard. Instead, she barely tapped his bottom six times. Then, A.B. sniffed. His hat was sitting whop-sided on his head.

I thought about that Mrs. Dunn told us everybody's name in the class was on the birthday train. But Mrs. Dunn didn't put her name up there. I wondered if teachers had birthdays. They might not. Or maybe Mrs. Dunn didn't want that birthday spanking!

Chapter 5

New Things Keep Happening

Mrs. Dunn told everybody to look at the wall that had all the windows. She said, "On the wall under the windows you can see I have a string that has clothespins hooked on it. We will be able to show your 'good work' papers hanging on that string." Then she told us to look at the counter that had a sink. It was on the back wall. She said, "We will be washing our hands before lunch. It is very important to kill the germs before we eat." Mama always told me to wash my hands before I ate at home, too. But I didn't know it was to kill something called germs. Mama didn't tell me why. She just said that I didn't need to eat with dirty hands.

Mrs. Dunn walked to a door that was right next to the sink. It was closed. She opened it and said, "This door is our connection to the other first grade class. In the little hall there is another door that is a closet. It looks dark in here because Miss Bohannan has her door closed. That way we will not disturb each other's class. But if I need to leave the classroom for any reason, I can open the door and Miss Bohannan can open her door. That way she can listen and watch you." I didn't know that Jimmy's teacher was named Miss Bohannan. I was glad my teacher had a shorter name for sure.

Levi asked, "Teacher, Teacher, when do we get to eat?" I reckon it didn't matter to Levi how short Mrs. Dunn's name was because he always called her Teacher anyway.

Mrs. Dunn told Levi that we would be going to lunch in about thirty minutes. She told the class that she was going to give everybody a new pencil. Then she picked up a box off her desk. She started at one end of the desks and she gave a brand new, really fat, blue pencil to each boy and girl. She placed it in the cut out part in the top of the desk. After everybody had a pencil, Mrs. Dunn said, "I know some of you have held a pencil and may even know how to write. But I want you to learn the correct way to hold a pencil." She walked around the class and made sure that everybody was holding the pencil right. She said, "Remember it is important to sit in your desk properly also. Your back should be touching the back, your seat should be in the seat, and your feet should be on the floor!" She looked at Levi. He scooted his feet to the floor. Mrs. Dunn kept checking the pencil in each kid's hand to be sure each one was holding it right. By the time Mrs. Dunn got to Levi's desk, his pencil already had teeth marks on it because he had been chewing on it.

By the time she got to A.B.'s desk, his pencil was missing. Mrs. Dunn asked, "A.B., where is your pencil?"

In his stopped-up-nose whine, slowly A.B. answered, "It's stuck in my shirt."

Mrs. Dunn said, "How in the world did it get stuck in your shirt?"

A.B. said, "Well, I used the pencil to try to scratch my back." He sniffed and then he said, "My back was itching really bad. And the pencil just sorta fell out of my hand and went into my shirt."

Mrs. Dunn told A.B. to stand up and she pulled the back of his tucked in shirttail out of his pants and got his pencil. She stuffed the shirttail back where it should be and told A.B. to try to hold on to his pencil better. She finished checking everybody's pencil.

"Okay," Mrs. Dunn said, "we will line up at the sink to wash our hands for lunch. When we go to the cafeteria, we will stay in line, and carefully carry a tray. At school you do not have a plate. You each will have a tray. It has little sections divided in it for the different foods of the meal. Our class will sit at a certain table. Mrs. Bohannan's class will be at another table. There will be other classes in there also. The teachers will be at a different table. Let's say our blessing and then we will go."

We walked down the hall and went into a big room with lots of long tables. The room had a stage at one end. When I turned the corner, I saw three ladies with nets on their heads and gloves on their hands. I saw Miss Myra. She was my Sunday School teacher when I was five years old last year. She always wanted us to behave at church. And in Miss Myra's class everybody did behave. She told us she would sit on us if we cut up. And Miss Myra was sorta fat. So we knew she would sqoosh us if she had to sit on us. I looked up and she said, "Well, hey there, Will. I see you are a big first grader now!" I smiled at Miss Myra. I figured the food must be pretty good if Miss Myra cooked it.

It was hard to hold that tray but I made it to the table. I felt sorry for Gillie because he dropped his tray and the food spilled all on the floor. That made Ethel start to cry. Virgil stepped beside Ethel. I heard him say, "Why don't you go home, Crybaby?" Then Ethel cried louder. Mrs. Dunn got napkins to clean up the mess. Then she got Gillie another tray of food.

A teacher that I didn't know came over to our table and told us to be quiet. This teacher looked old. She had a lot of lines and a heap of wrinkles on her face. She was kinda bent over when she walked too. I think she must have been at least fifty years old. I heard a boy at the table behind me say, "That teacher always makes her students eat everything on their tray. I heard that she says if they eat all the food, they will have nice skin and teeth and grow up strong and healthy."

Another boy at that table said, "Whew, either she didn't eat everything on her tray when she was little or it just didn't work on her!" The kids sitting at that table all laughed. I smiled. Then I looked at my tray and took a big bite out of my yummy hot dog.

Chapter 6

The Most Fun Part of the Day

After we ate our lunch, we took our tray to a window next to the serving line. The lady behind the window took the tray and turned it upside down. I was too short to see where she dumped it. We walked in line to the restroom and then back to our room. Mrs. Dunn said, "Everyday after lunch we will have a rest time. You will put your head down on your desk for a few minutes. Then I will read you a story."

I kept my head on my desk but I looked around too. I found out if you fold your arms on top of your desk to put your head on, it works better. As a matter of fact, I could see every boy and girl when I turned my head from one side to the other. Mrs. Dunn said, "You don't have to go to sleep, but everybody needs to close your eyes." I think some kids went to sleep because I heard some slow, heavy breathing sounds. And then somebody started snoring. I bet it was A.B. because of his stopped-up nose and all.

In just a little bit Mrs. Dunn said, "You may sit up now. I have a story to read to you." She sat in a chair at the bottom end of our horseshoe shaped desks. She showed us the picture book as she read it. "I want you to listen closely. This story is funny but it has a good lesson for you also." The story was about a little boy with a funny name. His name was Epami-something. I couldn't say it. I don't think that the boy was old enough to go to school yet. I know he wasn't smart enough. He always got mixed up about what to do with things. He was supposed to be taking different things from his grandmama's house back to his mama's house. But he messed up with the cake, and the butter, and the bread. And he almost drowned the poor little puppy. Every time his mama would tell him how to carry one certain thing, that's what he would do wrong with the next thing. I knew it was easy to forget stuff because I do that sometimes. But, he always forgot! After Mrs. Dunn finished the story, she said, "Now that you're in first grade you need to remember it is very important to follow directions at the right time. That is one of our main rules: 'Do what you are told when you are told to do it'!"

I thought about that I would ask Ida Claire about that story when I got home that afternoon. Mrs. Dunn might have told Ida Claire's class that same story when she was in first grade.

Mrs. Dunn said, "We will get to go outside for recess now. All six classes in the school will be outside. There are two sets of swings. The set closest to our exit door will be the ones you can use. The third graders use the bigger set of swings on the other side of the playground. Also, there are seesaws and a merry-go-round. And you will see monkey bars. They are the metal bars that are shaped almost like a castle. A tall slide is in the middle of the playground too. You may play on all of these, but be careful and hold on tight so you don't fall and get hurt.

We got in line and walked out into the hall. We went through the lunchroom, and the exit door, and then down the steps outside. Mrs. Dunn said, "When I stand up and raise my hand, recess will be over. You will need to get in our class line."

I went to the swings first. I looked at the other set of swings but I didn't see Ida Claire. There were a heap of boys and girls outside. Another little boy jumped in the swing beside me. He was in my class but I didn't know his name. He said, "You are in my class. What's your name?" I told him that my name was Will Lee. I asked him his name. He said, "My name is Grady Ponder. I'll get behind you and push you up higher in your swing. Then you can push me, okay?"

I told him, "I'll wait to the cat dies, and then I'll get out and push you."

Grady said, "What do you mean? I don't see a cat anywhere around here."

I told him, "My cousin Ida Claire said that if you wait until the swing gets slower until it stops completely, you call it 'wait till the cat dies'."

Grady said, "Okay, that's pretty good. I'll wait for my push after the cat dies for you." Then he laughed. I decided right then that I might have made a new friend.

Grady and I ran to the seesaws when we finished swinging. He got on one end and I got on the other. We

were just about the exact same size. So the seesaw was nice and even. One time we both stopped, picked our feet up, and the board was exactly balanced. We went to the tall slide next. It was a lot of steps up to the top. We each took a turn then ran to get back in line. Grady was at the bottom of the slide ladder ready to step onto the first rung. I was right behind Grady in line. All of a sudden Virgil came to the bottom of the slide ladder. He was pushing and shoving. He said, "Get out of my way. It's my turn." He climbed the rungs. When he got to the top, he flipped around the top safety bar, and then slid down the slide.

Grady looked at me and said, "That Virgil is a big bully." I nodded and knew for sure that Grady was my new friend. We each took our turn at the slide. Mrs. Dunn stood up and raised her arm in the air. We ran to get in line to go back to our room.

Chapter 7

What Did We Learn?

We were able to get some water from the water fountain in the hall. I sure was glad! I was about to thirst to death. Levi sprayed water all over his face. Then he used the bottom of his shirt to wipe the water off his face. When we got to our desks, Levi said, "Uh, oh, Teacher, I forgot to take Hoppy outside when we went to play."

Mrs. Dunn said, "Is that the name of your little pet frog?"

Levi said, "Yes'am, that's his name all right." Levi jumped up and ran to the back shelf to check on the box. Mrs. Dunn told him that she was sure that Hoppy was okay. So Levi went back and squatted on his feet in his desk.

Mrs. Dunn said, "Boys and girls, most of you played very nicely at recess. But, I want to remind you that you should always wait your turn and not push in line. That is an important rule so that none of you will get hurt. Also, no one needs to flip over the top safety bar on the slide. That is very dangerous."

I glanced at Grady. He nodded. We both knew that Mrs. Dunn was talking about Virgil Acworth. Mrs. Dunn said, "You will be learning many things this year in first grade. I know that today you haven't done very much actual work, but you have learned about some of your new classmates. You have learned about certain things in our room. You have learned about where places are located such as the restrooms and the lunchroom. You have heard about some of our rules. So when you get home today, and your mama asks you about what you learned, you can tell her.

Levi shouted, "I learned about where the playground is for recess."

Mrs. Dunn said, "That's right, Levi! Now, we have a few minutes before it's time to go home for today. Would anyone like to share and tell about something they did during the summer?"

Maggie Mae raised her hand. Mrs. Dunn called on her to talk. Maggie Mae said, "Well, one Saturday during the summer my family went to the zoo in Allbenny. I saw monkeys, and tigers, and ducks, and a big elephant."

I liked watching Maggie Mae talk. She moved her hands around when she described stuff. And I really liked to hear her talk. It was sorta soft and soothing. Every time she made the "s" sound, it was kinda like a hissing sound added to the word. I really liked that. As a matter of fact, I liked just about everything about Maggie Mae!

Grady told about the new dog he had. I listened carefully to hear about Grady's dog. I liked dogs and Grady was my new friend. He said, "My dog is a German shepherd. His name is Chief. We play together a lot. I live pretty close to the school so maybe one day Chief can come to school and y'all can see him."

Another boy named Nelson Gilmore said that he got to go to the circus that came to town. He said that he rode the elephant. I remembered going to the circus. Ida Claire and I rode that big elephant too. I remembered one boy fell off the back of the elephant. I really looked hard at Nelson to see if he was the boy. I decided he wasn't. Then Nelson said, "There was a little boy that fell off the back of the elephant and landed in a pile of poop. It got on his clothes and he really did stink." Everybody in the room laughed. At least everybody got tickled except Mrs. Dunn.

She said, "Settle down. Sometimes accidents happen. Well, our first day is almost over. Tomorrow we will begin learning our numbers and letters."

Levi said, "But, Teacher, I can't go home. I ain't learned how to read yet."

Mrs. Dunn said, "Well, Levi, you'll just have to come back tomorrow and see what happens."

Levi said, "Okay, Teacher, I'll ask Mama and see if she'll let me." He ran to the back shelf and grabbed the shoebox with Hoppy in it. "I need to take Hoppy back to his creek. He might get lonesome here tonight. I don't reckon you stay here at night, do you, Teacher?"

"No, Levi, I go to my home just like all the boys and girls do. But, I'll be back tomorrow." Mrs. Dunn said. Then she told us that the boys and girls that walk home would line up at the door first. I threw up my hand to wave bye to Grady. Four other kids went out the door. Mrs. Dunn told us that the kids that live in the country would be last because they would ride the bus. Shoot, I wish I could ride that big bus I saw outside the window. Then Mrs. Dunn said that the boys and girls that would be car pick-up could come with her to the outside door and wait our turn. As I walked out the door, I heard Levi say, "I hope my mama ain't mad at me 'cause I didn't learn to read today!"

Chapter 8

Afternoon Snack

I rode home in the car with Ida Claire and Millie. Millie was Ida Claire's best friend. And Millie's mama came in her Studebaker car to get us from school. I climbed in the back seat with Ida Claire. Millie said, "Will, how was your first day in school?" I told her that it wasn't as scary as I thought it would be.

As soon as I walked through the back screened door to the kitchen at my house, my Mama asked, "What did you learn at school today, Will?"

I said, "Nothing." I really knew I had learned some stuff but Ida Claire told me to come straight to her house after I saw Mama. I asked Mama if I could go to Aunt Ima's. Mama told me that I needed to change out of my good school clothes first then I could go.

When I stepped in the back door, I smelled a pound cake. Um-m-m-m! I loved warm pound cake. Ida Claire had on her shorts, too. She had to get out of her school dress as soon as she got home. She asked if I wanted a glass of milk to go with my slice of cake. I said, "Yeah, but I wish we had one of those little bitty glass bottles of milk that has the cardboard top lid like in the lunchroom at school. I never have seen one like that until today."

Ida Claire said, "I know. I don't like milk too much. But I like to drink out of those neat little bottles!"

Franklin came into the kitchen. He was Ida Claire's big brother. He was in eighth grade this year. He called us "Squirts" and usually didn't want to play with us. But, when it was time for a snack, he would talk to us while we were in the kitchen. Franklin said, "Well, Squirt, did you keep Mrs. Dunn straight this first day?" He grinned. He had been in Mrs. Dunn's class a long time ago when he was in first grade.

I told him, "Mrs. Dunn's pretty nice. We didn't have to do much work or anything. We just sorta found out about our classroom and about the new boys and girls and everything."

Franklin asked, "Well, do you have a new girlfriend now?"

I said, "There's one little girl that sure is pretty in my class. Her name is Maggie Mae. When she talks, it sounds soft and soothing. Her voice makes a hissing sound like the water lapping against a boat when we go fishing."

Franklin said, "It sounds to me like you're sweet on a girl that has a speech problem, Squirt!" And then he laughed.

I forgot that I was gonna tell Ida Claire about Maggie Mae first. I should have known that Franklin would tease me. But, I didn't care because Maggie Mae was worth it.

Franklin said, "I remember the first day I was in first grade. We were in a different building than what y'all are in now. We were on the back hall behind the high school. The windows were high up off the ground.

But Mrs. Dunn kept all the windows open so it wouldn't be so hot. There was a kid in my room that acted pretty scared the whole morning. His name was Arden Allen. I remember that about middle of the morning, Mrs. Dunn walked to the door and closed it. I never will forget what happened. When Mrs. Dunn got to the opposite side of the room to close the door, Arden decided it was time for him to leave. He made a mad dash and jumped head-first out one of the windows. He looked like he was doing a nosedive. We all jumped up and lined the windows looking out to see if he killed himself. But, just like a cat, he landed on his feet. He took off running. He must have lived pretty close to the school. By the time it was time for lunch, his mama marched him back into our room. She told him to stay with Mrs. Dunn until the end of the day!" We laughed thinking about poor Arden Allen.

We kept eating the yummy pound cake. Then, Franklin asked Ida Claire, "What happened in your class today?"

Ida Claire said, "Well, one of the things that was pretty good is that we have twin girls in our class. The funny thing is that their names are Ilene and Iona."

Franklin said, "So what! Why is that funny?"

Ida Claire said, "Their last name is Moore. Do you get it: Ilene Moore and Iona Moore?"

Franklin laughed and said, "Yeah, that's pretty neat I guess." Then he ran out the back door. The screened door slammed shut.

I didn't get it. The only thing that I knew about twins was that Ida Claire's daddy was a twin. I called him Uncle Ben. And when I was about four years old, his twin brother, Ida Claire's Uncle Rhen, came to their house. They looked exactly alike. When Uncle Rhen walked to the door of Uncle Ben's house, I told him hey. He just looked at me and told me that he wasn't my Uncle Ben. So the main thing I knew about twins was that they can get you real confused.

While we finished eating our cake, Ida Claire asked if I made any new friends. I told her about Grady. She said that she thought he might make a good friend. Then I told her about Virgil and how he acted.

Ida Claire said, "Yep, he sounds like your class bully for sure. Since I'm in third grade, we've known our bully for two years. He just gets a little sneakier every year. His name is Wilton Medford. All of the girls in the class always try to stay out of his way."

Grandmama came in the back door just as I finished my last bite of cake. I drank the last of my milk. She kissed the top of my head, then Ida Claire's. We knew that our Grandmama was the sweetest grandmama in the world. She lived really close to us. She told us that Mrs. Carr wanted us to come visit her when we got home from school. Ida Claire said that would be great. I asked, "Do I need to go tell Mama?" Grandmama said that my mama and Ima both knew we were going. So we each grabbed one of Grandmama's hands and started walking up the street.

Chapter 9

A Porch Swing is Great

Ida Claire and I always liked to go to visit Granny Carr. That's what all the boys and girls in the neighborhood called her. She was a really good friend of Grandmama's. One time Ida Claire and I talked about that Granny Carr was really old. Even Grandmama called her Mrs. Carr. Grandmama walked to visit her three or four times a week. She lived about two blocks from us and Grandmama said that she needed to do some walking as often as possible. Granny Carr stayed in a wheelchair. It was a tall, high-backed wooden chair with big wheels. I don't know why she had to stay in that wheelchair, but Ida Claire told me that she could not walk at all. She could move around anywhere in her house though and out on her big front porch, too. We liked the porch the best because it had a big swing at one end of it. Ida Claire and I climbed up in the swing and started rocking forward to make it move and swing higher. Grandmama sat in one of the porch rockers. And, of course, Granny Carr sat in her wheelchair.

She asked us if we had a good first day of school for the year. We both told her, "Yes ma'am." Then she stared up at the sky. She was thinking about something. That's the way she always did right before she told a story. Her stories were usually about when she was a little girl.

Then Granny Carr said, "A long, long time ago when I first started to school, I remember something that happened that very first day. We had many children in that room. We had grades that included first through sixth. We were all in the same room." I looked at Ida Claire. She was staring at Granny Carr. I could tell that she had not heard this story either. Granny Carr kept talking. She said, "We didn't have a lunchroom. As a matter of fact, that first day, my mama had put a biscuit wrapped in paper in the bottom of a little round bucket. That's what I took for my lunch."

Ida Claire asked, "Was that all you had to eat?"

Granny Carr said, "No, my mama had put some syrup in the biscuit and I had a pear from the pear tree in our yard." I looked at Grandmama and she nodded and looked back at Granny Carr.

Granny Carr said, "But the main thing I remember about that first day was that all the windows were open and all that morning a bird was whistling outside the windows. He was sitting in a dogwood tree just to the right of the schoolhouse. When the teacher told us it was time for lunch, I opened my paper and spread it out with the biscuit on top of it. Some of the crumbs fell on the paper when I picked up the biscuit to eat it. And just as I took a bite, that pretty bird flew through the window to my desk. He got a crumb off my paper and flew back and sat on the windowsill."

Granny Carr stared up at the sky again. She smiled and then she said, "My teacher told us that all of God's creatures need to eat!" I looked at Ida Claire and Grandmama. They had smiles on their faces just like I did.

Then Granny Carr told us that she had written a poem for us about school. She liked to write poems. She had read some to us before that she had written. I didn't know how anybody could write a poem. But she always made the last words of two lines together sound almost the same. Ida Claire said that was called rhyming words. She said that I would be learning more about poems in first grade. Granny Carr read her poem:

> When you're at school, you can have fun each and
>> every day,
> You'll read and do arithmetic as you learn and play.
> You may think: Will I be smart enough?
> Will this be too hard or be too tough?
> Can I keep up and do my best?
> Will I say what I should and pass all tests?
> And I say to you when I think about it;
> "This is what I know and you shouldn't doubt it:
> You'll have good grades after a small time to wait,
> But I know and feel that in school you'll do great!"

We clapped. Granny Carr smiled and said, "Well, that's the truth!"

Grandmama said that we needed to get on back home, but that we'd be back in a few days for another visit. Granny Carr thanked us for coming and told us to have fun every day at school. We waved good-bye and then grabbed Grandmama's hands to walk back home.

Chapter 10

Make a Wish

While we were walking home, Ida Claire said, "I'm glad I don't have to do any homework tonight. My teacher Mrs. Milton told us that we would start our homework in two or three days."

I asked Ida Claire, "Do you reckon I'll have to do homework in first grade?"

She said, "Yeah, but it's pretty easy in first grade. You'll have to practice writing your letters and numbers some. And then after you learn to read, you'll read a story at home every night for practice."

I told Ida Claire that I reckoned I wouldn't learn to read too fast. "We have a boy in our class named Levi. He thinks that he's gonna learn to read tomorrow. He talks sorta country, but he's pretty nice. And he's real funny. We got tickled at him a lot today."

Grandmama said, "Well, we're back at home now and it's about time for supper. So y'all go on in your houses and I hope you have another great day tomorrow at school." She patted our heads and told us good-bye.

I went in my house and Ida Claire went to hers. Mama told me to go wash my hands because supper was just about ready. As soon as I got through eating, I asked Mama if it was okay to go to see if Ida Claire wanted to play something. She told me that she would call me when I needed to come home to get my bath.

I went to Ida Claire's house. They were just finishing their supper. Aunt Ima had cooked fried chicken. It sure smelled good. But I was full. Franklin said, "Will, do you think Ida Claire can get the biggest part of the pulley bone?" Franklin and Ida Claire each grabbed one side of the pulley bone after they finished eating. The one that got the biggest part could make a wish.

I told Franklin, "I don't know if Ida Claire will get it or not. I bet she wishes she could so she could make a wish." They broke it. Franklin's piece was the biggest. I don't ever remember Ida Claire winning. Franklin should have had a lot of wishes come true by now! I reckon he won because he was older, and stronger, and smarter. So, he knew exactly where to grab to make it break right for him!

I asked them if they wanted to play some marbles before it got dark. Ida Claire said that she did. But, Franklin went to play some football on the field with the big boys.

We played marbles at our marble holes beside the cherry laurel bushes. I won one game and so did Ida Claire.

Mama called for me to come in. Ida Claire said, "Yeah, I've got to hurry and get my bath. My favorite TV show comes on Monday night. It's 'I Love Lucy'!" Ida Claire really liked that show. She did love Lucy just like the show name said. But Mama said that I had to go to bed at 9:00. And that's the time the show started. I told Ida Claire that I would see her in the morning.

The next morning I woke up as soon as I smelled that good bacon cooking. I went to the kitchen and sat at the table. Mama told me that she had my clothes hanging on the back of my bedroom door. So I ate breakfast and hurried to get dressed.

Aunt Ima drove Ida Claire and me to school that day, too. But this time she didn't get out and go to our classes with us. Franklin rode his bicycle with some of the boys that lived close to us. I thought about that if I ever got the longest part of the pulley bone, I would wish for a red bicycle. Of course, mine wouldn't be as big as Franklin's, but it would be neat to have a bicycle of my own.

Chapter 11

Confusing Words

After all the boys and girls got to school, Mrs. Dunn said that she was going to call roll. I didn't know what she meant. I looked to see if there was some sort of a ball or wheel that would roll. And I remembered sometimes that we had what Mama called rolls instead of biscuits. But it turned out to be different from what I thought.

She told us that she would say our name and we were supposed to say, "Here." That way she could tell who was at school that day. She pointed to the ABC's that were in a line on the wall above the bulletin board that had the animal pictures. "Both the way your desks are arranged and the way I will call roll are alphabetical. That means in ABC order," she said. Mrs. Dunn had used that "alphabetical" word a lot. But I didn't understand how Virgil could be first. The "V" was way down that ABC line. Mrs. Dunn said, "You are in order alphabetically according to your last name." Now that made sense because my last name was Lee and the "L" was in the middle of the ABC line. And I was about in the middle of the desks.

She held that register book. Mrs. Dunn called: "Virgil Acworth, Nina Combs, Marylou Cordell, Thomas

Deaton, Gillie Dunbar, Jeanette Evans, Nelson Gilmore, Harriet Hadley, Harvey Jeffers, Zeke Jones, Will Lee, Ethel Lewis, Abraham Manning."

Abraham said, "Here, my name's Abraham but everybody calls me Junior."

Mrs. Dunn said, "Is that right?" Then she called the next name: "Reba McFarley."

Just as Reba said, "Here," Levi came into the room.

He said, "I came back to school today. My mama told me that I could because she wanted me to learn to read. But, Teacher, I had to go to use that commode around yonder on that other hall before I could come to your room. I was about to get in a tight on the bus. Why are the boys and girls answering 'here' when you say their names? I thought everybody in our room could hear. Why are they telling you that?"

Mrs. Dunn cleared her throat and said, "Good morning, Levi. That is a different kind of 'here'. H-e-a-r is what you do when you listen with your ears. But, the children are answering 'here' spelled h-e-r-e because they are here at school today."

Levi said, "Oh-h-h, I'm glad I'm here and I'm glad I can hear, too!" All of us sitting in our desks smiled.

Mrs. Dunn kept calling the names: "Levi Mullins, Bess Patterson, Grady Ponder, Peggy Rhames, A.B.Seay, Janie Spelden, Lamar Tomlin, and Maggie Mae Warren. That's everybody in our class. As you see we have a few more boys than girls." Then Mrs. Dunn said, "We will have our Bible story and the Lord's Prayer as soon as I call roll each morning." She began by reading about Adam and Eve and the Garden of Eden. She told everybody to bow their heads and close their eyes. "If you know the Lord's Prayer, you may say it with me. If you don't know it, you can listen and keep your eyes closed."

After the prayer was over, Levi pointed to Zeke and said, "Teacher, that boy had his eyes open during your praying time."

Mrs. Dunn said, "And Levi had his eyes open, too!" Mrs. Dunn sure was smart. I knew Mrs. Dunn didn't peek. Franklin had told me that she had eyes in the back of her head. I reckon she could see with her eyes closed, too!

Mrs. Dunn said, "I think most of you have always lived in this town. But, is there anyone that used to live in another place?"

A.B. raised his hand. He sniffed. Mrs. Dunn asked him where he used to live. He answered more stopped-up sounding today than yesterday. He said, "I lived in Oh-wee County."

Mrs. Dunn looked puzzled, waited a minute, and said, "Where is Old Lee County?"

A.B. said, "No, ma'am, not what you said. It was down yonder in Brake-wee."

"Oh," Mrs. Dunn said, "You lived in Blakely in Early County."

A.B. nodded and said, "Yes, ma'am!"

Whew! Franklin thought that Maggie Mae had a speech problem! But I knew that A.B. really had one. I was amazed again that Mrs. Dunn could figure things out so good.

I hadn't noticed Bess in our room yesterday. I reckon there was just too much stuff going on to remember everybody. But Bess was my cousin. It was far down the line. Ida Claire said that when she asked Aunt Ima about it, she told her we were third cousins. She said that some folks called it first cousin twice removed. I just knew that we were kin somehow. I remembered one time when Bess and her two brothers came to Ida Claire's house to play. Their Mama brought them one day when it was raining. So, we played inside the house. One of the games we played was "Blind Man's Bluff." Bess and her little brother would get so tickled because Ida Claire would always feel their nose and ears to guess who it was. In that game the blindfold made you have to touch and listen really good. But the funniest thing to all of us was when Bess and Ida Claire would put on a show. Ida Claire would put her hands behind her back. She had her arms tucked in close by her sides. And Bess would hide really close behind Ida Claire and stick her arms and hands out acting like they belonged to Ida Claire. Bess couldn't talk. She could only pretend to be Ida Claire's arms and hands. One time Bess took a banana, peeled it, and stuck it in Ida Claire's mouth. Another time Ida Claire pretended to sneeze. Bess grabbed a Kleenex and put it over Ida Claire's mouth. Then she used the Kleenex and pinched Ida Claire's nose together for her to blow her nose. We got on the floor

laughing because it was so funny. Arnold, Bess's older brother told them to go watch in the mirror. Bess and Ida Claire really got tickled then.

I must have been doing what Mama called day-dreaming. I heard Mrs. Dunn say, "We will learn our numbers. I have a story to help you remember each one." Shoot, I missed what Mrs. Dunn said before that. But it was fun to think about that day at Ida Claire's house. And I was glad that Bess was in my class, too!

Chapter 12

One and Won

Mrs. Dunn went to the blackboard and with a piece of chalk she made a straight line. She asked, "Does anybody know what that represents?"

Over half the class answered, "That's a 'one'." But Levi said that he thought it was a straight stick. I couldn't believe that a few kids really didn't know what it was. I knew my numbers all the way to twenty. But those other kids hadn't played school with Ida Claire as much as I had.

Mrs. Dunn said, "This is how we write the number 'one'. And I want you to think about this story when you practice your numbers: Once upon a time a little boy named Johnny always stood straight and tall. We will pretend that this straight line for 'one' is Johnny standing straight and tall. When you write it, be sure to start at the top of your line on the paper and keep it straight and tall as you go down to the bottom red line. Also, put your finger after it so you can skip a space before you make another one. You may practice now."

We all started writing our "ones". I heard A.B. sniff and I heard Levi sigh. I reckon some of the boys had never tried to write numbers before today. Mrs. Dunn walked around checking each desk and looking to see how we were doing.

When she was on the other side of the room from Virgil, he mumbled,

"Any baby can make a silly 'one'!"

Then Nina said, "Mrs. Dunn, Virgil said that a baby can make a silly 'one'!"

Virgil gave Nina a dirty look and called her a tattletale!

Mrs. Dunn called for the class to pay attention. And she said that it was not necessary for anyone to be talking. Then she told us that she wanted us to make two lines of the number 'one' for homework. I wondered if she gave us homework because she got mad about Virgil and Nina. She said that we would find out more about Johnny as we learned how to write the other numbers.

Then Mrs. Dunn started on the letter "a". She explained that an "a" was made with a ball and a short stick touching it. She said that an "a" was a vowel. I thought it was just a letter. She went on to say that an "a" can make two different sounds. It depended if it was a long "a" or a short "a". Levi said, "Teacher, I didn't know that a letter could make a sound at all!"

That was one time that I thought Levi made some sense. Mrs. Dunn said that sometimes it was confusing, but we would learn more about letters every day! Then we practiced writing the letter "a". This time Mrs. Dunn let us go to the chalkboard and take turns writing it.

After we finished our morning work, Mrs. Dunn said that she wanted us to know about our helpers each week. She explained that we would have a leader. We would have other helpers, too. One person would get to empty the pencil sharpener. Another person would get to erase the board. She said that there would be other "helper" jobs added later. She explained that we would have the same job for a whole week. She also said, "But, each one of you will be responsible for your own desk. I don't want your desk to look like a garbage can. And we certainly don't want such a mess that a little mouse could come to live there." I heard all that she said but I was thinking about that I wished I would be picked to erase the board for a whole week. I knew that would be really neat to do that! It turned out that she picked the helpers in alphabetical order. So, Virgil got to be the first leader. Nina would empty the pencil sharpener, Marylou got to hand out stuff, and Thomas was the lucky one that got to erase the board every afternoon before we went home. I guess it would be a long time before Mrs. Dunn got to my name for any job.

We worked hard all morning. Before I knew it, we had gone to lunch, had rest time, and then it was time for recess. At recess almost half the class decided to play the game of Red Rover. Maggie Mae said that she knew a good way to pick the captains for the two sides. She told everybody to get in a circle around her and she would do "acka, backa". Ida Claire, Millie, and I had done this a bunch of times with some other kids at the house. About ten of us were in a circle around Maggie Mae. She pointed to a different kid each time she said a word.

She said, "Acka, backa, soda cracker, acka, backa, boo; acka, backa, soda cracker, out goes you!" Ethel stepped back. Maggie Mae started again and did the "acka, backa" several more times. It turned out that the two kids that were left to be the captains were Grady and Junior. They each started calling names to be on their side. Grady picked me first. I was really glad. We took turns choosing. When it was my turn, I picked Maggie Mae. I remembered how to play this. Junior's team got to call first. They said, "Red Rover, Red Rover, send Ethel right over." Ethel ran but she didn't break through. So she had to stay on Junior's team. It was our team's turn to call. We called Jeanette. But, she didn't break through either. So we got to keep her on our side. We were still tied. It kept going until our team had more. When the other team called Grady, he broke through and was able to bring one back to our team. I was able to break through for my turn, too. We were having fun. Then Virgil ran up to the other team. He got in the middle and said that he wanted to play, too. He stood between Junior and Lamar. He yelled at them to do the double arm lock. He told them what that meant. We watched. He grabbed the arm up above the wrist and locked his fingers tight and told Lamar and Junior to do the same. Then their team said, "Red Rover, Red Rover, send Gillie right over." Usually the boys could break through. But, Gillie was sorta sissy. He ran with his arms flapping and flying in the air. And he looked more like a chicken prancing instead of a boy running.

Virgil said, "Come on, Four Eyes." When Gillie tried to run through the arm lock, Virgil raised his arm up and caught Gillie in the face. Gillie flipped backward. His glasses came off and his nose started bleeding. We looked up and Mrs. Dunn was walking quickly toward Gillie. Virgil mumbled, "Sissy's shouldn't play. We won!" And he went to the swings. A bunch of us helped Gillie up and got his glasses for him. Mrs. Dunn called for Virgil to come to her. She had watched the whole thing. She took Virgil by the arm and marched him to sit beside the teachers for the rest of recess. Grady, Maggie Mae, and I grinned at each other.

Grady said, "It looks to me like we won in more ways than one!" Yep, today turned out to be a good day at school, too!

Chapter 13

Learning More Stuff Everyday

Everyday we had more stuff to learn. Mrs. Dunn said that we had gotten into what she called a routine. I didn't know exactly what she meant. But, I did know that we did almost the exact same thing at the same time everyday. The part I liked best during arithmetic time was the story that Mrs. Dunn told about the numbers. Everyday we learned a different number with a different story. She had already told us about the number "one" being little Johnny standing straight and tall. Even if I hadn't already learned my numbers, I could have learned them pretty quickly with the neat story. The story with the number "two" was that little Johnny was walking home from school and saw a pretty swan swimming in a lake. The number "three" story was that little Johnny saw an airplane in the sky with lights on it. When little Johnny went to sleep at night, the first part of the "four" was made for the headboard and flat part of the bed. Then, the next morning when his mama called him to get out of bed, little Johnny sat straight up on the edge of the bed and put his feet on the floor. That made the last part of the number "four". The story that made number "five" was that little Johnny went on a diving board, jumped straight down, and then swam around.

The number "six" was made because little Johnny got in a hurry and stumped his big toe. I remember the day that Mrs. Dunn told about the "six". When she finished showing us how that "six" looked, Levi said, "Whew! That big toe sure swoll up big!" I had stumped my toe before and I knew it sure did hurt bad when you stumped your toe. We learned about the number "seven" next. Little Johnny was leaning on a table so hard that part of one of the legs broke off and that made the number "seven". Mrs. Dunn told us that it was beginning to get really cold where little Johnny lived. She said that the pond where the swan was, had frozen over with hard ice. So, the boys and girls could ice skate. When they did skate, they showed Johnny how to go in two little circles that connected and made the number "eight". And after many days of learning our numbers and practicing writing them for homework, we finally got to the number "nine". The story ended because little Johnny wasn't so little anymore. As a matter of fact, Johnny finished school and joined the army. He became a soldier with a pack on his back for number "nine". Mrs. Dunn told us that it was important for Johnny to stand up straight and always be sure that his backpack was closed up at the top.

We worked hard learning our numbers for many days. I was also able to learn more about the boys and girls in my class. During those days Virgil was always a bully. Nina stayed busy being a tattletale. But it was usually about something that Virgil had done or said.

Ethel finally quit crying everyday. Levi kept his feet in his desk instead of on the floor where Mrs. Dunn said they belonged. I still thought that Maggie Mae was the prettiest girl in our class. But, I noticed there was another little girl in our class that couldn't keep her feet still. Her name was Harriet. She was the shortest one in the class. Every time I looked in her direction, I saw her feet were swinging or stepping in the air. I watched her face. She looked like she was thinking real hard about something. Day after day Mrs. Dunn would say, "Harriet, you need to be still. You are disturbing the other boys and girls." And Harriet would stop moving her feet for a few minutes. Then before you knew it, she would start back.

One day while we were in line at the water fountain, I heard Maggie Mae ask Harriet why she kept moving her feet. Harriet said, "After school started, my Mama put me in a dancing class. My dance teacher told us to practice everyday. So, while I'm at my desk, I do: 'shuffle, hop, step' with one foot and then the other. Then I do: 'shuffle, step, and shuffle, step, step' with each foot." Maggie Mae said that that explained everything! It didn't make much sense to me. But one thing was for sure – Harriet was practicing everyday a lot!

The very best thing that happened after we had been in school for a month was that one of my bottom front teeth got loose. I wiggled it with my fingers and my tongue. Just as soon as I got home, I told Ida Claire about it the first day that I noticed it. She told me that it would take a few days to come out. Then I'd be able to put it under my pillow for the tooth fairy to get it and leave me some money. I wanted to get some money so I had a steady job keeping that tooth moving. I remember one time when Ida Claire lost a tooth. It bled a long time. I hoped mine didn't bleed. I wasn't crazy about blood coming out of my own body especially! I got that tooth loose enough that it was hanging by just one little corner. Franklin told me to bite into the apple he handed me. I did. And that tooth stuck in that apple. I put the tooth under my pillow that night. The next morning it was gone but I had a dime in its place. I asked Mama at breakfast if I could pull out some more teeth that day. She told me that they would fall out when they should.

When I went to school, I grinned at everybody. Grady asked me what the tooth fairy brought me. Virgil walked by and said, "You look stupid to me, Snaggletooth." He sure did like to be mean to everybody! I wondered if he lost his teeth like normal kids or if somebody had knocked his out. He already had his big teeth coming in. But, I didn't get to keep thinking about that too much. Mrs. Dunn was ready for us to get busy learning more stuff that day!

Chapter 14

Getting Ready for a Holiday

The week after we had been in school for six weeks, we took home a report card. Mrs. Dunn called each kid's name to come to the front of the class and get his card. She told us that we could look at it first then put it in our book sack. She said, "If you see an 'S' in the first line, that means that you are doing Satisfactorily. You will need to get your parent to sign the report card on the back of it and bring it back to school tomorrow."

Everybody looked at his own report card. I had all S's on mine. I felt pretty good about that. When I looked at Maggie Mae, she was smiling, too. Levi asked, "Teacher, what does 'N' mean?" She told him that the letter 'N' meant that someone needed to improve in a certain area. Levi said, "Oh." I heard Virgil mumble that 'N' meant "not too smart!" Nina opened her mouth to call Mrs. Dunn's name, but Mrs. Dunn cleared her throat and said that it was time to be dismissed.

When I got in the car, Ida Claire asked if I had a good report card. I told her I did. She said that she had gotten all A's. She told me that the letter "S" was as good as an "A". She said that she liked getting the first report card because that meant that we would start decorating for Halloween soon. Ida Claire told me that since I was in school now, I would really learn how much fun holidays could be.

Sure enough, by the end of that week Mrs. Dunn let us draw big orange pumpkins. She changed the "animal talk" bulletin board to ghosts and black cats. It said, "Don't Be Scared-Say BOO To Adding". We had already started practicing the "plus zero" and "plus one" facts. And those were printed on the bulletin board, too.

The next week we made all kinds of decorations for our room. We drew and cut out black witches' hats and black cats. She let us trace around some patterns she had. We made yellow eyes and teeth in orange jack-o-lanterns. And we made white ghosts. Mrs. Dunn told us that we would have a Halloween carnival on Halloween night. It was supposed to be at the baseball field up the hill from the school. She told us that each class would have two booths. Our parents and P.T.A. people would come to work at the carnival. Some parents would be able to send things ahead of time. I knew that Mama would probably cook something like cookies to send ahead.

At the first of the week Ida Claire and I started talking about what we would dress up like for trick-or-treating. We talked about different costumes we could make. Ida Claire asked Aunt Ima if she had some stuff she could use to be a gypsy. Aunt Ima said, "That's a good idea. I have an old skirt and blouse you can wear. I have some beads for your necklace and a scarf we can tie around your hair. You'll make a good gypsy!"

Ida Claire asked me if I wanted to be a hobo. We knew that would be easy. When we asked Mama, she told us that she had an old mop that we could use the handle for the stick I would carry. She said that I could use one of Daddy's red bandana handkerchiefs to tie to the end of the mop handle. She said that I could wear some really old clothes and shoes. Ida Claire said, "Yeah, Will, you get to put dirt on your face, too!" That all sounded pretty good to me. I never had been able to get dirty on purpose. The day before Halloween, Franklin used Uncle Ben's saw and cut the mop handle for me. When he cut it, I heard Mama tell him that it was time to buy a new mop anyway.

That Friday finally came. It was Halloween! We never had homework on Friday. And we were going Trick-or-Treating and to the Halloween carnival that night. After we got home from school, we had our snack. Grandmama came in the back screened door and asked Ida Claire and me if we wanted to go visit Mrs. Carr with her. We asked Aunt Ima and Mama if we could go. They told us we could.

We walked with Grandmama to Granny Carr's house. Part of that time we were skipping around Grandmama because we were excited about that night. Granny Carr told us that she had written a Halloween poem for us. Then she read the poem:

During the season with a scary scene,
The witches and wizards make Halloween!
There are ghosts, goblins, and goonies galore

With masks, monsters, magicians, and more.
Costumes come in all sizes both large and small-
All fit many children - whether short or tall.
That night you pick who you may want to be
Dress up as that person, so all may see:
You could be a doctor, a good one for sure
One that is famous with a wonderful cure.
You could be a teacher with an apple and chalk-
But where are your students, did they leave you and
    walk?
Be a pirate with a patch over one eye-
With a sword and an "Argh", we will hear you cry.
You could be a witch with a hat and a broom
If you scream when you run, others will make room!
A girl can be a princess with a very pretty dress.
Boys might be hoboes with a face that's a mess!
Whatever you choose, it's fun to trick-or-treat,
And have a bag full of candy that's yummy to eat!

After she finished reading the poem, we clapped.
She wanted to know what we would be dressed up as
that night. She said that she wanted to be able to rec-
ognize us when we came to the house for candy. We told
her about our costumes. Then we started home. When I
looked at Ida Claire, I could tell that she was just as
excited about that night as I was!

Chapter 15

Halloween Fun

We got all dressed up and ate our supper in a hurry. We each grabbed a brown paper bag. Aunt Ima told Franklin that he would walk us around the neighborhood to go trick-or-treating. Franklin knew he was too old to actually go up to the doors of the houses to say "trick-or-treat". We told him we would share our candy with him. He told us that he knew where his buddies Oscar and Henry were hiding. They were in certain places just to jump out and scare little kids. So, when we got to those houses, Franklin warned us about it. We didn't get too scared. Ida Claire and I sure were glad that Franklin was looking after us so good. And we were glad to give him some of our candy when we got home.

We saw a bunch of other folks trick-or-treating, too. Sometimes we knew who it was and sometimes we didn't. The hardest ones to identify were the ghosts. They had an old white sheet on them with the eyes cut out. I never did know a single ghost I saw.

The last house we were going to was a two-story house. Franklin said, "Did y'all Squirts know that the old Edwards' house is haunted?" I asked him what "haunted" meant. He said it meant that it had ghosts.

Ida Claire asked me if I remembered the ghost story that Aunt Ima told us one afternoon. I did remember it. Ida Claire said, "You know Mama told us about the house that had an old woman that had died twenty years before that time. So you see that house in Mama's story had a ghost and it was haunted."

Ida Claire and I both looked at each other. We really didn't want to go to that door of the Edwards' house. She said, "Franklin, we've got enough candy. Let's just go on back to the house so we can go to the Halloween carnival at the school." I nodded because that sounded like a great idea to me. We went back to the house and dropped off our brown bags of candy.

Aunt Ima took us to the carnival. There were different games set up all around the baseball field. Some men had put up wooden frames and then put burlap bags on them to divide them into different little rooms. We walked all around looking at all the choices of games to play. Ida Claire and I each had fifty cents. That meant we could do five different games. Ida Claire saw Millie. She was dressed like a ballerina dancer. I think she used her dancing costume. I saw Grady. He told me that he wanted to be a zookeeper and let his German shepherd dog, Chief, come to the carnival. But, his mama told him that Chief might tear up stuff. So Grady came as a pirate. He had a black patch on his eye. I saw A.B. He was dressed like a cowboy. Then I saw a clown. It turned out to be Gillie. Maggie Mae was a witch. But, she wasn't an ugly witch with a wart or green hair. She was like the good witch on the Wizard of Oz.

Ida Claire said that she and Millie wanted to "bob" for apples. Grady and I went over to the Fish Pond. We "went fishing" and each got a prize. I decided to do the "ring toss". I was able to ring two of the bottles so I got another prize. Ida Claire went in the Fortune Teller booth. She came out and said, "Will, you ought to go in there. That fortune teller is really smart."

I went in her booth. She had a veil on her face and a lot of jewelry on her hands and fingers. She told me that I had a sister that lived in Atlanta. She said that my daddy worked for the railroad and that he liked to go fishing. She told me that I had a cousin named Ida Claire. Whew! That fortune teller sure knew a lot of stuff about me. Then she said very slowly, "I see in my crystal ball that you can throw a baseball quite well! And I see you riding a new, big, red bicycle. Now, the vision is growing dim. That is all I know for now." When she said that, I knew I was supposed to leave. So, I went out through the curtains.

Boy, I really got my dime's worth from that fortune teller. I couldn't wait to tell Ida Claire about my new red bike. Maybe I would get it for Christmas. That fortune teller knew about everything else so I was sure she knew about my bike, too.

Franklin came up to me. He had been on the hayride. He asked if we had any more money. We each had a dime left. He said, "Good, we'll all go in the Scary Booth last. I'll stay with you so you won't be too scared."

When we went in, a grownup put a blindfold on our eyes. He said, "Okay, put your hand in this bowl. You will feel eyeballs. Now put your hand in this bowl. It is blood." A lady told us to give her our hands after that bowl. She said that she needed to wipe the blood off our hands. The man said, "Put your hand in this bowl and you will feel intestines—your insides!" Then he said, "Put your hand in the last bowl. You will feel a brain!"

Yuk! I didn't like that booth. I was glad when they took off the blindfold and we could go back to the regular carnival. Aunt Ima met us outside that booth and told us that it was time for us to go home. Ida Claire asked Franklin about all the stuff we felt. He told us that the eyeballs were really grapes. He thought that the blood was ketchup. He decided that the intestines were really spaghetti. And that a sponge was for the brains. I was glad that Franklin set us straight on all that stuff. He sure was smart.

Ida Claire said, "Franklin, I think you peeked and looked out under your blindfold."

Franklin grinned and tapped the side of his forehead and said, "Naw, I've just got a good sponge for brains!" And we all laughed.

Chapter 16

Duty Calls

When we went back to school the next week, things had settled down. The ghosts, black cats, and jack-o-lanterns were all gone from the classroom. The best thing I found out was that it was my job to erase the board for the week. I knew I could do my job good and that I would be a great helper. I knew that sometimes some of the boys and girls didn't do too good at their jobs. When it was Gillie's turn to empty the pencil sharpener, he didn't do too good. He tried to shake the left over pencil sharpener shavings out into the trash can. He shook and shook but they wouldn't all come out. Mrs. Dunn said, "Gillie, hit the side of the trash can!" So, Gillie held the pencil sharpener up in the air with one hand and hit the side of the trash can with his other hand. He looked kinda confused. Mrs. Dunn had a little smile and said, "Hit the side of the trash can with the pencil sharpener and it will get cleaned out, Gillie!"

Gillie said, "Oh." Then he did what Mrs. Dunn told him.

Since we had been in school, we had learned almost all the big capital letters and all but one of the little small letters. We did printing in first grade. Ida Claire told me one time that I would learn to do real writing when I get to second grade. I was having enough printing practice with my homework. It seemed to me that most of the letters were made with a ball and a stick. As a matter of fact, that's the way Mrs. Dunn taught us. Some letters just had taller sticks than others. And some letters were not a complete ball. They were just part of a ball, like the letter "c". We would sing the ABC song everyday for practice. After we had practiced for weeks, Levi told the class, "I know all my ABC's. I can even say them backwards." Before Mrs. Dunn could stop him, he jumped out of his desk, turned around backwards from everybody and sang the song all by himself. I looked at Grady and we both grinned.

I remembered when Mrs. Dunn told us about the monkey tails on the "j", "g", and "y". Another set of tricky letters was the candy cane for the "f" and the humps for the "m", "n", and "h". The day that we learned the last letter, Mrs. Dunn asked, "What do Nina, Thomas, Jeannette, Nelson, Harvey, Zeke, Ethel, Levi, Bess, Peggy, A.B., and Janie have in common? In other words, what is the same about these names?" Nobody could guess. She told us, "All these boys and girls have the letter 's' either in their first name or last name." So that day we learned that "s" stood for a crooked snake. And that was the day I started to get to erase the board. So I was really glad when Mrs. Dunn made everybody take turns practicing the letter "s" on the blackboard. I was able to show Mrs. Dunn that I was the best blackboard eraser helper that she ever had.

It rained the next day. That was the first time it had rained during recess. So we had singing time in the room. The leader for the week got to pick the first song. Harriet picked, "Strut Miss Lizzie." Girls liked this one. I think it was because each one could be prissy going down the line. The boys got on one side in a line and the girls got on the other side facing the boys. We all stood shoulder to shoulder in the two lines. Harriet started the walk between the two lines. She put one hand on the back side of her head and the other hand on her opposite side hip with her elbow sticking out. Then she changed hands as she strutted. We were singing the song while she went between the two lines. The boys would do it too, but they would try to show off and act goofy. At least nobody would make fun of anybody else because each of us was going down the lines when it was our turn.

Harvey picked the next thing for us to do. He chose "The Farmer in the Dale" for us to sing. He got to be the farmer first and picked a wife. Each kid picked the next one like the song said to do. Finally the cheese stood alone. This time it was A.B. Since he was last, he chose for the next game to be "Simon Says". We had just gotten started good when Mrs. Dunn said that recess was over.

I was glad that it had stopped raining by Friday. When we had recess time, a bunch of us played what we called "Monster Tag". We pretended that one person was the monster. If he caught anybody, they had to go to a room in his monster castle. Each square in the monkey bars represented a room where you stayed until someone came to rescue you. That was a great game.

Some of the girls loved to play "horses". I saw Marylou, Jeannette, Ethel, Reba, Peggy, and Janie playing this. All the girls had sashes on the backs of their dresses. During recess time they would untie the pretty bow and use the sash like it was reins to the bridle on the horse. So there were three girls that were the horses and three girls right behind them holding on to the sashes. The ones in the back would say, "Giddyup!" And they would take off running. It looked like it was fun.

But that Friday afternoon something even more fun happened. Since I had been board eraser all week, I got to go outside and dust the erasers. We had been taught that the one that did it correctly could hit the erasers together, or they could beat the tree close to the corner of the building. But, we had been told, under NO circumstances were you supposed to beat the erasers on the side of the building. So, I dusted those erasers exactly as I should. I took them back inside and gave them to Mrs. Dunn. She smiled at me. I was proud so I stood up a little bit taller. She told me that I had done a great job all week. When I climbed in the car that afternoon, I felt happy that I had done my best as a board eraser helper.

Chapter 17

An Old Bus

That next Saturday it was raining again. Ida Claire called and asked if I could come to her house to play. I asked Mama and she said that I could go. When I got to Ida Claire's house, she was watching television. The picture on the TV was black and white. Franklin unrolled a piece of plastic film he had. He said that Uncle Ben brought it home from a store. The top part of it was blue. The middle was green, yellow, and red all mixed together, and the bottom was brown. It was the exact size of the TV screen. Franklin stuck it on the front of the TV and, all of a sudden, we had a TV that was showing colors. It was like magic. It was amazing! We had never seen anything like that. We watched the TV all morning. Sometimes the horses on the cowboy shows looked green but the sky was always a pretty blue color. I couldn't wait to see my favorite cartoon in color. But I would have to wait to the next holiday. The Captain Kangaroo show didn't come on Saturday or Sunday. And the cartoon I liked best was on the Captain's show. It was Tom Terrific and Mighty Manfred the Wonder Dog. I figured it would be really fun to watch that in color!

We had a peanut butter and jelly sandwich for lunch. Franklin left to go to one of his friend's house. Ida

Claire asked me, "What do you want to play next?" I told her that it didn't matter to me. We decided that we would play "bank" for a little while. So Aunt Ima gave us some tin foil and we got the scissors. We cut little circles for dimes. We made middle-size circles for nickels and bigger circles for quarters. We got some plain white paper next. Then we cut little circles and colored them brown for the pennies. Then we cut rectangles and colored them green for the dollars. We made like we were buying and selling all sorts of things.

When Aunt Ima was through cleaning up in the kitchen, she came and sat down in a chair in the living room where we were playing. Ida Claire said, "Mama, can you tell us a story about when you were in first grade?"

Aunt Ima said, "Yeah, y'all younguns are sights always wanting to hear stories about the olden days."

I asked Aunt Ima, "What do you remember that happened when you were in first grade like me?"

Aunt Ima said, "Well, one thing I remember was about the bus we rode. It was different from buses today. This bus was a Model T Ford and the body of it was made out of wood. It didn't have regular glass windows. It had openings on both sides of the bus. Some canvas material was attached to the top of the openings. When it was hot weather, the canvas was rolled up and hooked at the top. That way we could get a little breeze. In the winter the canvas was tacked at the bottom. The seats on the bus were long, wooden, plank benches that ran all the way down both sides of the bus under the window openings.

The benches had a little padding on them and the back we leaned against was just the side of the wooden bus. There was a long wooden bench in the middle of the bus, too. There were some poles that helped to hold the middle bench in place. Since we lived way out in the country, we were almost the last children to be picked up by the bus driver. I remember that we always stopped at Miss Anderson's house after the bus was just about completely full. Miss Anderson was my first grade teacher and she didn't have a car. So, she was glad to ride the bus so she didn't have to walk to school. Everybody on the bus tried to crowd together a little bit closer to make room for Miss Anderson. I loved my teacher. She was a short, plump little lady. She sat down at the end of the side bench on the only empty space available. It wasn't as wide as she was! The bus started again on the bumpy dirt road. We were all bouncing where we sat. Then in a high, precise little voice, Miss Anderson said, 'Well, I think I am sitting on a little bit of nothing!' I was tickled but I was too scared to laugh out loud. Then the whole bus load of kids howled and laughed because they were so tickled."

Ida Claire and I laughed at Aunt Ima's story, too. I wish I could have seen that bus. It sounded pretty neat.

Ida Claire asked, "What else do you remember, Mama?"

Aunt Ima said, "Well, one afternoon we were going home from school. We had a substitute bus driver. One of the girls in the back of the bus was playing with some paper. She hollered for the bus driver to look at the picture she had drawn. He looked up in the rearview mirror. When he did, he lost control of the bus and it hit a sand bed on the side of the road. The bus started swaying and rocking from side to side. It was a hot day so the canvas material was rolled up to the top. Now, your Uncle Jim realized that the bus was probably going to turn over. So he jumped and went sailing out the window opening. He landed in the peanut field and then ran to get out of the way of the bus. You know Jim is four years older than I am. He was right! Sure enough, that bus wrecked and turned over on its side in the field. The kids in the bus had been tossed and flung all around from one side to the other. There were arms and legs flouncing. Kids were screaming and yelling! When that bus flipped on its side, it splintered because it was made of wood. I was little so I sat in a little ball with my arms hugging my legs. Pieces of wood and splinters were all around and on top of me. I was really glad when Jim found me and pulled me out. I wasn't hurt. A few kids had cuts and scratches though." Aunt Ima smiled and asked us what we thought about that bus story.

We told her that we really liked it and asked her to tell us some more stories of when she was in first grade. Aunt Ima said, "I remember a few more stories but I've got to get back busy working here in the house. Y'all were really good listeners!"

Ida Claire and I talked about how great it would have been to be able to ride in a bus made out of wood. Then, we started back playing "bank" because it was still raining outside.

Chapter 18

The New Boy

Monday started a new week of school. We had learned what Mrs. Dunn wanted us to do everyday. She told us that our routine was firmly established now. And she seemed pleased about that. That day she passed out shiny little flat blue books to us. She said, "These are Blue Horse composition books. You will use these for your spelling tests for the next twelve weeks. On the front you can see a blue horse in an oval shape. These little coupons can be collected to send in to get books for our classroom. We will not cut them out until the composition book has been completed. Now, write your name on the outside cover. Remember you will only use these for your spelling test each Friday." We had been having spelling tests since our first report cards went home. We had been using plain paper for the test. I liked having spelling tests. Ida Claire practiced my words with me for homework. She was a really good speller. I remembered asking her one day if she had the "spelling angel" when she was in first grade.

I thought about that she said, "Yeah, Mrs. Dunn always made us close our eyes and put our heads down on our desks. And the 'spelling angel' would go around and grade our tests. Afterwards, Mrs. Dunn would tell everybody to sit up straight and open their eyes. Then she would walk around looking at the test. She would call out the kids' names that had made 100 on the test. We would all clap for them!" I was glad that the 'spelling angel' still came to our class, too. I realized that I was doing what Mama called daydreaming. So, I started back paying attention to Mrs. Dunn.

After we learned about our new blue horse spelling books, we worked on adding facts for arithmetic time. We had learned a bunch of facts already. Today we were doing a test that had fifty facts on it. We had reviewed the plus zero, plus one, plus two, plus three, plus four, and plus five facts. Mrs. Dunn gave out the paper and told us to do our best. Everybody started working. And, if they were like me, they were thinking real hard. Mrs. Dunn went to a bookshelf behind the door. All of a sudden there was a knock on the door. Mrs. Dunn opened the door. We looked up and saw the principal of the school standing there with a boy and another woman. The principal said, "Mrs. Dunn, this is Herman Suggs. He is your new student. And this is his mother."

Mrs. Dunn shook hands with the boy's mother. Then, she said to the boy, "We are glad you will be in our class, Herman. Come in and see your new friends. Boys and girls, you may stop your test and meet our new student."

Herman stepped through the doorway. His hair hung even with his eyebrows. The hairline had a gap cut in the side above his right eye. He smiled at the class. I saw that he was missing one of his top front teeth. But the other tooth in the front was the biggest tooth I had ever seen. It was as wide as my thumb, I thought. He waved his hand to us like he was cleaning a window going round in a circle. We had already learned about shapes. And I didn't want to be mean, but I thought to myself—his head looks like a triangle. The top part was big and wide and the bottom of his face had a very skinny chin. He was tall and lanky. Mrs. Dunn closed the door. She said to us, "Everybody, tell Herman hello!"

Herman said, "My name's Herman, but you can call me 'Skinny', 'cause you can see that I'm tall and skinny!" When he talked, it sounded like he had a wad of cotton stuffed in his mouth. He talked loud, too! And he kept his mouth open all the time. I think that big front tooth was sticking out too far for his lips to touch together.

We were excited to have somebody new in our class. Levi started bouncing on his feet in his desk. He said, "Teacher, Teacher, can Skinny sit next to me?"

Mrs. Dunn said, "No, Levi, we have to get him a desk first. Herman, you may sit at the reading table and look at the books while the boys and girls finish their arithmetic facts test." She pulled out a chair for Herman to sit in and motioned to him to stay quiet and look at the books.

Mrs. Dunn told us to get back busy working on the facts test. She went back to the bookshelf. All of a sudden, Herman jumped up and ran across the room to Mrs. Dunn. He pulled on her dress and said, "Did you know my

cat died? He scratched me right here on my arm right before he died." And he pointed to the scratch. Mrs. Dunn turned around and had a different kind of look on her face. I think she was shocked. Before she could say anything, Herman fell to the floor. He stretched out, then stuck his left leg and left arm up in the air. He held them up stiff-like. Then he said, "This is what my cat looked like when he died!"

It was so quiet in the room that you could have heard a pin drop. Mrs. Dunn looked around at everybody in the class. She cleared her throat. Then, she said, "Herman, I am sorry that your cat died. But, you must be quiet while the students are working. Get up off the floor and go back to your chair."

Herman got up, walked back to his chair shaking his head from side to side. He said, "Yep, that's what he looked like when he died. He was a mighty fine cat, too!"

I wasn't sure, but I thought to myself that Herman was going to have a lot of new rules to learn in our class. And I was pretty sure that Mrs. Dunn thought now that our routine wasn't so firmly established since Herman was in our class!

Chapter 19

New Clothes Can Be Trouble

The next Monday morning before I got out of bed, I heard Daddy say to Mama, "Well, Miss Sophie, feels like we're having our first cold snap this fall." I knew that Mama was standing at the stove cooking bacon and eggs for breakfast. And I knew that Daddy had just pretended to pinch Mama on her backside. He always did that when he called her 'Miss' Sophie.

Then I heard Mama say, "Stop that, Hiram!" And she laughed. Mama called to me, "Get up, Will, it's time for you to get ready to go to school. You can wear those new blue jeans today since it's kinda chilly." I rubbed my eyes, yawned, and then went to the breakfast table.

When I got to school, I saw a bunch of the boys had on new blue jeans, too. The jeans really were stiff and scratchy, but they were warmer. Mama had rolled the cuff up about three times on each of my pant's legs. I noticed the girls had on sweaters this morning, too. I looked at Maggie Mae. Her sweater was light pink. She seemed mighty proud of that pretty sweater. I heard her tell Ethel, "Mama bought me this pink sweater and she said I could wear it to school today if I didn't get it dirty." Ethel told her that she liked Maggie Mae's sweater, too.

Mrs. Dunn began class by calling the roll from that register book. We answered "Here" like we should when we heard our name. We always worked on spelling first. Mrs. Dunn called and wrote each spelling word on the board.

I glanced at Maggie Mae. She looked pretty in that new pink sweater. I saw her brush off one sleeve and pat it. Then she started brushing the other sleeve. She stopped and stared at something on the wrist of that sleeve. Then I noticed she pulled it a little. It was a thread and it got a little bit longer when she pulled it. I was watching Maggie Mae and Maggie Mae was watching that thread getting longer.

Mrs. Dunn asked, "Maggie Mae, what are you doing?"

Maggie Mae said, "Nothing."

Mrs. Dunn said that everybody needed to be paying attention. "You need to watch and listen to be able to spell your spelling words for this week." Mrs. Dunn told us three more words. I watched her write those words on the board. Then I glanced at Maggie Mae. That string from her wrist of her sweater was getting longer and longer. She started a little pile of the string in one place beside her wrist. By the time Mrs. Dunn finished telling us all the spelling list, Maggie Mae had a pile of thread about the size of an egg. Mrs. Dunn said, "Maggie Mae, what are you doing?"

Quick as lightning, Maggie Mae jerked that thread pile and both hands under the top of her desk. She said, "I'm paying attention, Mrs. Dunn. The last spelling

word you said was 'good'. G-o-o-d spells 'good'." I don't know how in the world Maggie Mae knew that last word. But I did know one thing-she did really 'good' to know that word!

We had all our other regular lessons before lunch. Then, after rest time, it was time for recess. Mrs. Dunn told us, "Men came during the weekend and paved the road around the back of the school. It is asphalt. You will walk straight across the black asphalt to get to the playground. Do not play near the asphalt." I knew I had smelled a funny tar smell all morning. But I didn't know it was called asphalt.

We went outside and walked straight across the asphalt like Mrs. Dunn told us to do. Then when we got to the dirt, we took off like a bunch of wild Indians. That day Harvey asked if I wanted to play with him at recess. I asked him if he wanted to go to the seesaw first. So, that's what we did. Then, we went to the swings. Then, he remembered that he had a little rubber ball from home stuffed in his blue jeans' pocket. We started bouncing and throwing the ball back and forth to each other. On the hard clay part of the playground the ball bounced okay. When it hit a little piece of gravel, that ball bounced crooked and rolled across the asphalt and out of sight. The teachers sitting on the porch couldn't see where the ball went. Harvey took off after the ball. When he got on the other side of the asphalt, he realized that the teachers couldn't see him. He waved his hand and motioned for me to come there.

I made sure that the teachers were talking. Then I ran to where Harvey was. We bent down on the edge of the asphalt and Harvey reached down to pick up some of the little left over black pieces. He said, "Feel this, Will. It's kinda soft." I got a piece in each hand and mashed it. We could shape it like a snake or a cigar. Then, we took some little pieces and made round little marble balls. Harvey said, "It's getting hotter outside today. That's why we can make different shapes."

About that time, Mrs. Dunn called, "Recess is over. Everybody needs to line up!" Harvey said that we ought to keep some of the shapes to take home. I told him that we couldn't put them in our pockets because they would poke out.

Harvey said, "I know. Let's unroll the cuff on our blue jeans and put the stuff there. Then we can roll the cuffs back where they were."

I said, "Shoot, yeah! That's a good idea. But we've got to hurry and get at the back of the line." We went back in the room. I could smell tar every now and then. But nobody knew about it except Harvey and me. Mrs. Dunn read us a chapter from *Pinocchio*. When it was time to go home, I looked at Maggie Mae. That one sleeve of her sweater was up to her elbow. She took off the sweater and crammed it in her book sack. She didn't look too happy. I heard her tell Ethel that she didn't think that her mama was going to like her sweater now.

Chapter 20

"T" Stands for
Trouble and Thankful

I got into trouble at home the day that Mama washed that pair of blue jeans. She called to me while she was standing in front of the washing machine. When she showed me the cuffs, she asked, "Will, what in the world happened to these jeans?"

Uh, oh! I had forgotten all about the asphalt. I told Mama about what happened. Then I said, "Harvey told me to do it."

She said, "If Harvey told you to jump in a fire, would you do that, too?" Then she told me NOT to play with Harvey anymore. She said, "If you ruin your clothes again, you'll be getting a switching to help you remember to take better care of things."

I told Mama, "Yes, ma'am."

I guess I wasn't the only one that got in trouble. When Maggie Mae wore that pink sweater the next day, both sleeves were at the elbow. Ethel asked her what happened. I heard Maggie Mae tell Ethel, "My Mama cut off the other sleeve and told me that I needed to remember about taking care of my clothes."

Mrs. Dunn had changed the bulletin board again. This time it had turkeys and the words WE ARE THANKFUL.

She told us that we would write a word to name something we were thankful for and that piece of paper would be placed on the board, too. She said, "We are getting ready for our next holiday. It will be Thanksgiving. During this week we will make pine cone turkeys and learn about the Pilgrims and Indians."

Levi bounced in his desk and said, "Teacher, are you gonna talk about cowboys and Indians? I love to play 'cowboys and Indians'."

Mrs. Dunn said, "No, Levi, the first Thanksgiving took place before cowboys were alive." Then Mrs. Dunn said, "First, I will give you a big piece of paper. You will spread out your fingers and lay your spread-out hand flat on the paper. With your writing hand, you will trace around the flat hand." She showed us how to do this with her hand on the black board so we all could see the right way to do it. Then she showed how to connect and draw feathers and the head for the turkey. She said, "When you have completed your turkey drawing, you may color it. We will hang the pretty pictures on the line under the windows when you are finished."

I heard Gillie say, "I like drawing the stick-like legs and feet to help the turkey stand up better." Gillie was a good drawer. Mrs. Dunn said that he was an artist.

Virgil Acworth said, "I reckon Four Eyes can see how to draw better because of those glasses he wears." Mrs. Dunn told Virgil to be quiet!

That week we also learned a song to sing for Thanksgiving. The words in the song were talking about

going over a river and through some woods to get to Grandmama's house. I was glad that my Grandmama lived close to me.

The last day before Thanksgiving holidays was exciting. Grady lived close to the school so he walked to school every day. That day his German shepherd dog, Chief, came to school with him. A bunch of us played outside with Chief until the bell rang. When the bell rang, we said, "The bell, the bell, the B-E-L-L, bell." Grady told Chief to go home and we went in to Mrs. Dunn's class. That afternoon when we went outside for recess, Chief was at the playground. A bunch of us played with him and had fun.

Virgil went up to Grady and shoved him. He was so sneaky though. He always made sure that the teachers were not watching him when he did something mean. Virgil almost knocked Grady down. He said, "I guess you think you've got a good dog, huh?" Before Grady could answer, Chief growled and barked at Virgil. Chief started going towards Virgil. Virgil looked around and ran to the slide. He climbed up to the top thinking that he was safe. Everybody at recess stopped playing and started watching Chief and Virgil. Everybody knew that he was such a big bully! Then Chief climbed those steps on the slide ladder, too. Then Virgil slid down the slide. He probably thought that Chief couldn't do that. But, Chief slid down right after him. Virgil took off running and went into the school and closed the door fast. We laughed and rooted for Chief. He couldn't open the door, but he stood there barking until Grady pulled him away. The teachers didn't try to stop Chief. I reckoned they knew what a bully Virgil was. Maybe they thought he got what was coming to him.

Ida Claire's class was at recess, too. So, she got to see the whole thing. When we got in Millie's Mama's car that afternoon, we were all still laughing about it. While we ate our afternoon snack at Ida Claire's house, we told Franklin about it. He said, "That serves the bully right!"

Grandmama came in and said that she was going to visit Mrs. Carr. She said that we could go, too. We didn't have any homework during the holidays. And we always liked to visit Granny Carr.

When we got to Granny Carr's, she asked us if we wanted some cookies. We had already had our snack, but we could always eat another cookie. Since Granny Carr was in a wheelchair, she had a cook come to her house every day. The cook was Lula. And Lula had made peanut butter cookies. They had those fork stripes criss-crossed on top. And they were really good to me.

Granny Carr asked, "Did y'all have fun this short week at school? Did you make a pine cone turkey?" Ida Claire and I both told her that we had. Granny Carr said, "I've written another poem that I would like to share with all of you."

During this season, many thanks we give
For all the blessings each day that we live.

We're thankful for books that we read that plant
    a seed
With wonderful thoughts and instructions to heed.
We can appreciate things in just a blink,
We have good homes and good minds to think,
As I sit each day and look above,
I know so many blessings of love.
Family and home that we have this special day;
Enjoy wonderful food and watch the kids at play.
At this time our many blessings we share
To let others know that we really care.
Of all the things—I'm thankful for friends I see
    face-to-face.
Knowing each one of you makes this world a better
    place!

We clapped. Grandmama told us to tell Mrs. Carr thank you for the cookies and the poem. We did and then we walked home. The next day was going to be Thanksgiving. I knew that meant some more good food to eat. It also meant that we would have a heap of fun playing with all our cousins!

Chapter 21

Christmas Lights and Our Party

My sister Hannah came home from college to visit for Thanksgiving. Since Ida Claire lived next door, she got to my house before all the others did. But, by dinner time my aunts and uncles and all eight cousins came. We got to eat turkey, dressing, ham, sweet potatoes, green beans, butter beans, corn, pear salad, potato salad, and rolls. Of course, the desserts were really good. Ida Claire picked lemon meringue pie to eat. And I ate my favorite – chocolate cake. After we ate, we went outside to play. It was cold but the sun was shining. Right before dark, all the out-of-town cousins left to go home. Aunt Ima's family and mine had leftovers for supper. Ida Claire and I each had a good turkey sandwich. As soon as it got dark, Uncle Ben told us to get on our coats. He said that it was time for us to ride to town. I asked Mama if I could go. She told me that I could. So, Uncle Ben, Aunt Ima, and Hannah rode in the front seat. Franklin, Ida Claire, and I piled in the back seat of the car.

On Main Street Thanksgiving night, the Christmas lights were first turned on to start the Christmas season. And as soon as we turned the corner to be riding down Main Street, there those lights were. They were shining so pretty and bright that I just about lost my breath. The lights were blue, red, green, orange, and yellow. The strings of lights went from one side of the buildings on the street all the way over to the buildings on the other side of the street. And it was string after string all the way down the street. When we rode down the street, Uncle Ben said, "Y'all roll down the windows and stick your heads out and look up!" I could see that the colored bulbs were big just like regular light bulbs. And there were so many! I was so excited I just kept my mouth open wide. My heart and stomach felt like they were playing "leap frog" inside of me.

Ida Claire said, "I love getting to see the lights. They are wonderful! When I see the lights, I know that Santa Claus will be coming in a few weeks." I nodded.

We had fun the next few days playing outside. Sunday was the day that Hannah left to go back to college in Atlanta. When she was leaving, she said, "Will, you and Ida Claire need to get ready to be my helpers when I come home for Christmas. I will need both of you to help me wrap the presents I bring home."

We told Hannah, "Okay, we sure will be ready!"

When I went back to school that Monday, the turkey stuff was all gone from the room. The bulletin board had a picture of Santa Claus on it. It had the words HE'S MAKING A LIST on it, too. I looked carefully to see whose names were on that list. I saw my name. I think everybody's name in the class was there. Yeah, even Virgil Acworth's name was on it. If his name was there, I knew all the others would be. Maybe Virgil would be better since Chief had gotten after him. I think all the boys and girls were glad to see each other. There was a lot of talking and noise in the room. Maybe they had seen the lights and were still excited like me.

Mrs. Dunn said, "I hope each of you had a wonderful Thanksgiving. We will be decorating and doing things to get ready for Christmas. But, we also will do our school work each day."

So, we started practicing our facts again during arithmetic time. During reading time we found out that Dick, Jane, and Sally had a cat named Puff. We read all about Puff. Mrs. Dunn had changed some of our desks to different spots in the room. They were still in the horse-shoe shape. But, she had Levi, A.B., and Gillie sitting in a little group by themselves. Mrs. Dunn had to spend extra time with them every day. She had put the new desk for Herman right there with those other three boys. I reckon she thought that Herman would fit in pretty good with them. I thought she was probably right.

During that week we made Christmas wreaths. We decorated pine cones to look like little Christmas trees. We drew string lights zigzagged on paper trees and colored different bulbs to help decorate them. After we had lots of colored balls added, we colored and cut out those green trees, too. We really stayed busy the next two weeks before the Christmas holidays.

Mrs. Dunn read us different books about Christmas. She read the book about the night before Christmas. She read another story about a little mouse talking to Santa. When she read what the mouse said, she made her voice sound high and squeaky. Levi said, "That mouse sounds just like my little girl cousin when she talks!" Grady and I looked at each other and smiled.

The last day before Christmas holidays, we had our school Christmas party. Mrs. Dunn put a Christmas record on the record player. We sang along with the music. My favorite song was "Jingle Bells". I heard Maggie Mae say that she liked "Santa Claus is Coming to Town" the best. The grade mothers came to the classroom after lunch. They set up a pretty table with a big glass bowl full of punch. We had Christmas cookies, potato chips, and all kinds of candy. Each kid had a cup for the punch. The ladies told us we could have more punch in our cups if we were thirsty. Herman must have loved punch. He would hold his head straight back, turn that cup up, and drink that whole cup of punch at one time. I don't reckon that his big front tooth got in the way for that. I think he got four more cups of that punch. He ate three platefuls of party stuff. But as soon as he took one swallow of his fifth cup, he poured the rest of it back in the punch bowl. He said, "I'm through now. I had a plenty. No need in wasting what's left over!" The lady standing at the punch bowl tried to stop him. But, he was too fast.

We all decided that we were through, too! The ladies gave us all a red and white candy cane and told us "Merry Christmas!" Mrs. Dunn gave out the little orna- ments we had made. They had our school picture on each one of them. We told each other "Merry Christmas" as we walked out the classroom door.

Chapter 22

Christmas Rides

As soon as I got home I showed Mama my picture ornament I made. She told me that she liked it and to just put it on top of the TV. She said that I would be able to hang it on our Christmas tree the day that Daddy got it put up in the living room.

The next day Aunt Ima asked Mama if I could go with them to Allbenny to the Sears store. She said that I could. I remembered going last year at Christmas, too. It seemed like a long way to Allbenny. We rode for a long time. But, we finally got there and went into the store. As soon as we went through the doors of the store, we could smell the good smell of chocolate coming from the candy counter.

The best part of the Sears store was the escalator. I remembered that I was really scared of those moving stairs when I was four years old. Aunt Ima told us to always be careful not to let our toes get caught when you got to the top. So, Ida Claire taught me to jump off when it came to the end. Sometimes I wondered where I would go if my toes got caught and it sucked me under the floor. But, I tried not to think about it too much. I just made sure that I jumped high enough not to get caught.

That day Aunt Ima told Franklin to stay with Ida Claire and me. Uncle Ben said that he was going to the

tools section. Aunt Ima told us that she would be in the clothing section. We went walking around the store. We took turns riding the escalator up and then walking to the other side of the second floor and riding down on the escalator. Franklin told us to come with him to another part of the store. We walked by the place that had all kinds of bathroom samples. There were sinks, cabinets, and commodes of different colors. Each section had a wall separating it from another part. One section had all pink things. Another bathroom was blue. Another sink and commode was tan. Ida Claire said, "Just look at all the different colored commodes."

Franklin called to us to come look around the corner. When we looked at the white set, we saw a little boy. He looked liked he was about three years old. And he looked like he was tending to business. Since that commode was white, I reckoned he thought it looked like his bathroom at home. He was sitting on the commode with his breeches at his ankles. Franklin said that we needed to get back to the escalator. I asked him, "Why?"

Franklin said, "That kid must have been in a tight. But, the way he's propped with his arms straight and his face so red, he means business!" Sure enough, in just a minute, we knew by the smell! We didn't smell the good chocolate from the candy counter any more! We all three took off running and found Aunt Ima. We laughed and told her all about it.

Aunt Ima said, "His mama needs to be watching him more carefully." Then she smiled, too.

Franklin said, "Yeah, what do you think they'll do when he tries to flush it and it doesn't work? I bet the store workers will really be surprised!" We all laughed again.

By the time we left the store, it was dark outside. We got to see all the pretty lights and decorations in the town. Uncle Ben rode us on some streets that had lights at houses, too. Ida Claire said, "I'm tired of turning my head to be able to look at both sides of the street. Wouldn't it be really good if our eyes were where our ears are on each side of our heads?" I laughed and everybody else in the car did, too!

Chapter 23

Christmas Trees and Memories

The Saturday before Christmas Eve, Daddy said, "We'll go to the woods today and cut down our Christmas tree for the house. Will, go ask Ida Claire and Franklin if they want to go, too." I grabbed my coat and ran out the door. That screened door slammed, but I was too excited to wait to catch it like I was supposed to do. I ran into Aunt Ima's house. I was jumping up and down and almost out of breath.

Aunt Ima said, "Is there a fire somewhere, Will? Slow down and catch your breath."

I told Aunt Ima about what Daddy said we were going to do. Franklin and Ida Claire both looked at Aunt Ima hoping she would say it would be okay for them to go. She nodded and told them to bundle up good because it might get colder.

When we went outside Daddy was putting his saw and some rope in the trunk of the car. He closed it down and told us to get inside the car. We did. We rode way out in the country to some woods. When we stopped, Daddy got out of the car and went to the trunk. He grabbed his saw and said, "We'll spread out some to search for the right tree. But, walk so you can still see everybody. We don't want anybody to get lost." We started walking and we started looking.

Ida Claire found a cedar tree and hollered, "Look, Will, come see if you like this one." I told her that it looked too tall for our house. So, we kept hunting together. We saw a few squirrels. But, we didn't have to worry about snakes because the weather was too cold.

Franklin yelled, "Uncle Hiram, I think I've found the perfect one." All of us walked to where Franklin was. He was right. It was shaped pretty and was nice and fat at the bottom. Daddy got on his knees and started sawing. In just a few minutes Franklin said, "Tim-ber!" And the tree fell to the ground.

Daddy let Franklin and me grab the trunk and drag the tree back to the car. Ida Claire said, "I can't wait to help decorate it." We always helped each other decorate our Christmas trees. Daddy tied the tree on the top of the car and we headed home.

Mama had a spot cleaned out in the living room. Daddy nailed a wooden "x" on the bottom of the tree trunk. He placed the tree in front of the window where it would stay. Mama had gotten down the lights, balls, ornaments, and icicles. We got busy. After the tree was all decorated, Daddy held me way up high so I could put the star on the very top. Daddy said, "Plug her up and let's see the best tree in town." Franklin plugged in the lights. Ida Claire and I stared and opened our mouths. Then we clapped. It was so pretty. We both said, "Wow!" Ida Claire said that she would be glad when they got their tree up tomorrow. We sat down on the couch and kept looking at the tree.

Franklin went back to his house. Mama went to the kitchen. Daddy went outside to the car. But Ida Claire and I kept sitting and kept looking at my wonderful Christmas tree.

I said, "I don't know how in the world I will be able to go to sleep tonight. As far as that goes, I don't know how I'll be able to go to sleep for the next five nights. Because that's when Santa Claus comes."

Ida Claire said, "I know what you mean. But, I've found out if I think about funny things that happened at school, I can go to sleep quicker."

After I took my shower that night, I got in my bed. But I was wide awake and still excited. Then, I remembered what Ida Claire told me to do. So, I started thinking about funny things from school. I thought about Chief, Grady's dog, chasing Virgil up the slide. I thought about Herman spread out on the floor showing Mrs. Dunn how his dead cat looked. I thought about the Halloween carnival. I thought about playing Red Rover at recess. I thought about A.B. and his stopped up nose that made him sniff all the time. And I thought about Levi. I remembered how he came in the room with that bullfrog in his hand that first day of school. And I thought about Maggie Mae in that pink sweater with the short sleeves. Ida Claire was right. I didn't have anything to be scared about in first grade. School was fun! And funny things happened all the time. I took a slow, deep breath. My eyelids were closed. I smiled a little smile and went to sleep.

**To order books or schedule a school visit
please contact Kay Heath at
kayheath@mchsi.com
229-995-4055**

Ida Claire, It's Summertime! $10.00 includes tax

Ida Claire, That's Funny! $10.00 includes tax

Ida Claire, That's A Mystery! $10.00 includes tax

Three Little Frogs in a Boomerang Journey $16.00 includes tax

S&H cost $1-$25 is $4.00
                   $25 plus is $8.00

www.KayHeathBooks.com

Kay's books are available online and may be purchased via credit card at: Georgia SouthWestern State University Campus Bookstore.